Trapped in the Past

Dian Taylor

Contents

Chapter 1

A loud scream followed by a gunshot jolted me awake.

My heart was pounding rapidly inside my chest as I sat on my bed, terrified. All I wanted to do was curl up in a ball under my covers and hide from all the bad things that were taking place outside my room.

But my mom and dad were out there, and I knew they would allow nothing to hurt me. So, with shaky hands, I slowly pushed the covers away. Then I grabbed my teddy bear and held it tightly to my chest, hoping that it would bring a little comfort to my heart.

Mom and Dad must be watching something scary on TV... I thought as I turned the doorknob and walked out of my room. My whole body was trembling as I walked slowly on my tiptoe into the unknown.

When I reached the stairs' railings, my eyes widened in fear at what I saw. And suddenly, my chest tightened, making me feel as if I had completely forgotten a simple task as breathing.

Forcing my body to move, I hid quickly behind a nearby wall and peeked at the scene in front of me.

There were four masked and armed men surrounding something that I could barely identify as they were hiding it by their tall and muscular figures.

Where are Mommy and Daddy?

That was all I could think about as I tried to take slow and deep breaths to keep myself calm. I couldn't do anything that would make those men find out that I was here, watching them.

My dad once told me that if I ever found myself in a dangerous situation, I should never interfere and just call 911 and ask for help. I knew I should do that, but I couldn't bring my legs to move.

One intruder moved, and I gasped, dropping my teddy bear to the ground. I clasped my hand over my mouth once I saw what they were hiding with their large bodies. I moved my eyes away quickly, trying to grasp what I just witnessed.

I knew it couldn't be real. It was only a bad dream. It would be all over soon and then I would hide in my mom's arms, knowing that nothing could ever hurt me.

I took another glimpse at the scene, for my brain refused to believe what I saw the first time. There was a lifeless body on the floor; it belonged to a woman whose blood was scattered everywhere. That woman was no one but my mother...

My dad was kneeling on the floor, holding her body in his arms. His sobs echoed through the house. He shouted something that I couldn't identify at the masked men, but it earned him a punch in the stomach. He growled in pain and fell to the ground. They told him something, but he wasn't listening to them anymore, because he was looking straight at me with his hazel eyes that always made me feel safe.

Tears were falling like showers from my eyes, making it blurry to see and my whole body was trembling so hard that I couldn't move an inch. But despite all of that, I managed to stay silent, so they failed to notice that I was there. I locked my eyes with my dad for a couple of moments, then I watched as his lips parted, forming the word hide.

But it turned out to be a very hard task because my whole body refused to comply; I was frozen in my place, completely paralyzed. I just stood there watching in horror as one man approached my dad and put a gun to his forehead. There was a strange tattoo on that man's hand that was holding a gun. It looked like a foreign symbol. He leaned in and whispered something to my dad.

My dad focused his eyes on me for a couple of seconds before he looked him in the eyes and spat something at him. The man with the tattoo groaned loudly and pointed his gun once again in my dad's direction.

"I believe you already miss your wife, Agent Ryan," the man said in a malicious tone. "Tell her I send my regards."

He pulled the trigger, and the gunshot echoed through the house. It was like a time machine button that turned everything into slow motion.

The nefarious smell of gunpowder was now lingering in the air. And I watched as my father dropped to the floor. His eyes were wide open, and blood was gushing with sickening determination like angry falls from the wound on his forehead, forming a pool around his body.

I stood silent for a couple of moments, trying to take in what had just happened.

Yeah, it must be a horrible nightmare. I should have listened to Mommy after all. I shouldn't have watched that crime movie before bed...

Yet, I knew that something was wrong, because if it were really a dream, then why wasn't I waking up?

My heart hammered in my chest as I felt a rising panic. And suddenly, I felt as if all the air was being pulled vigorously out of my lungs.

I couldn't take it anymore. I screamed my lungs out, and immediately, all heads turned to where I was standing. The man with the tattoo said something to his partners, and they started walking toward me.

Backing off, I ran as hard as I could without looking back and locked myself in the closet in my room. I hugged my legs and waited for them to break in and kill me—but for some reason, they never did.

Then, I heard sirens coming from everywhere, and shortly after that, the police found me.

I was in shock when they found me, and I couldn't utter a word. I was traumatized. All I could think about was the sound of screams and gunshots, and the smell of blood and death.

And I kept longing for the moment when I would wake up from that dreadful nightmare—but it never came...

Waking up with a gasp, I panted as I tried to push away the remnants of the nightmare I just had. I pulled up my trembling hand to wipe the cold sweat that had formed on my forehead before I ran my fingers through my hair.

It has been a very long time since that day, yet that nightmare felt so real. And the fact that every minor detail of what happened was still carved in my memory didn't help either.

However, having that nightmare, especially today, didn't surprise me that much. Tomorrow was a very important day for me as it would be my first day as an official FBI agent...

Looking at my nightstand, I huffed in annoyance. There were three hours left until my alarm was supposed to go off, but I knew that I could never drift back to sleep, especially after that nightmare.

Pushing the covers away, I slipped from the bed and made my way to the kitchen. And as I was pouring myself a cup of water, a gentle breeze of air tickled my face, making me notice that one of the windows was left open.

I was about to close it when the breathtaking view of the streets of Manhattan caught my eye. New York was one of the busiest and loudest cities in the world; however, that was one of the many things that made it even more irresistible. It was the city that never sleeps, after all.

Tucking a piece of hair behind my ear, my mind drifted back to the nightmare I just had.

I always used to promise my younger self that I would let nothing break me or bring me down no matter what. That I would grow up to be the woman my parents always wished to see, and that I would do whatever it took to make them proud.

All the years I had to spend without my parents weren't easy, to say the least. But I always knew they must be watching over me from above, and because of this, I kept pushing myself forward every time I felt like giving up. I tried to hide the scars that day left on me as hard as I could, but no matter how hard I tried, I still felt trapped inside the memory of that incident.

Growing up, I always had this fantasy of catching the cold-blooded murderers who took my parents away from me. And maybe that was why I always dreamed of being an FBI agent, following in my father's footsteps.

The rest of the family, of course, disagreed. They said my parents got murdered because of my dad's job; however, I didn't listen to them. I remembered my dad's commitment and dedication to his job, justice, and restoring order. And I always wanted to be like him—as brave and strong as he was.

Also, I really believed in justice, even though I never had it myself, and I knew how much that hurt. So, I thought that helping other people have their own justice would help ease that pain a little.

I took a long, deep breath and sighed, then I looked at the clock on the wall. I still had a couple of hours before having to get ready for work, and I really needed a distraction, so I decided to do some workouts.

After I finished, I took a quick shower, then I started getting prepared for my first day.

Deciding to go totally formal, I put on a white shirt, a charcoal gray blazer, and slacks of the same color. Then, I put my gun into its holster after making sure it was loaded.

I checked myself one last time in the mirror. My long dark-brown hair was neatly styled in a bun updo. And I had forgone all makeup, so the only thing that pointed out my fair features was my chocolate brown eyes.

I smiled at my parents' framed picture that was on the mounted table before I grabbed my keys and left the apartment.

It took me about twenty minutes to arrive at the FBI headquarters at the Federal Plaza. I parked my car and got out. I looked at the huge building in front of me for a couple of seconds, feeling a little in awe. This was the beginning of everything I dreamed of, ever since I was a little kid.

Shaking my head a little, a smile made its way to my lips.

The Federal Bureau of Investigation, here we go...

Once I was in, all my stuff had to go through an X-ray machine, and I went through a metal detector. Then a security guard stopped me and asked to see my badge. I showed it to him with a proud smile, and he typed something on his computer, probably checking my name on the database. I was new here, after all.

I had to wait for a few moments before a slight smile made its way to the guard's face. "Welcome on board, Agent Ryan."

I thanked him with a genuine smile before I proceeded toward the elevators. In the elevator foyer, there were pictures and descriptions of the FBI's Ten Most Wanted. And there was a signage board that had the three words that captured the essence of the FBI in bold lettering. Fidelity. Bravery. Integrity.

The ding sound that meant my elevator had arrived brought my attention to it; I got in and pressed the tenth-floor button. But before the door closed, a guy with light brown hair and hazel eyes stepped in. He was about to click on the tenth-floor button too, but stopped when he noticed I had already done that.

"Oh, are you going to the violent crimes unit too?" he asked with a smile.

"Yes."

"Are you by any chance the new agent?" His eyes lit up as he threw in another question.

"I am," I replied with a confident smile.

"I'm Caleb Woods." He held out his hands to me. "I also work there, but not as a special agent, though. I'm a technical analyst."

I was usually a good judge of character and he seemed like a really nice person, and I immediately started to like him. I shook his hand back with a smile. "Alexandra Ryan, but you can call me Alex."

"Nice to meet you, Alex." He smiled. "Welcome to our team."

I shared the smile. "Thank you, excited to be part of it."

The elevator stopped and both of us stepped out. The floor was full of agents sitting at their computers and others walking here and there. Some were running with files in their hands probably to get signatures for different warrants, and others were escorting handcuffed felons.

"Hey, why don't you let me introduce you to the rest of the team?" Caleb suggested.

"Okay, why not?" I agreed with a shrug. I really needed to know the people around here, anyway.

I walked beside him until we were standing in the middle of the bullpen. He stopped and pointed at me. "Hey, guys! Attention, please," he started speaking at the top of his lungs. "Please help me welcome our new agent, Alexandra Ryan."

Blinking a few times, I was taken aback by his unique way of handling the introduction. I opened my mouth a few times, trying to find the right words while the entire office was staring at me. "Um... hi. It's going to be a pleasure working with all of you."

Some of them sent me welcoming smiles, while others just ignored me and continued with whatever they were doing before being interrupted by Caleb.

"What an introduction." I looked at Caleb with a smirk on my face.

He grinned sheepishly, rubbing the back of his neck.

I noticed a woman with green eyes and brown-reddish hair who seemed around my age approaching us. "Hey, I'm Ava Smith. I'm one of the communication liaisons in this unit," she introduced herself. Then she beamed at me. "Finally, more girl power in here. As you see, this place is full of testosterone."

Letting out a small chuckle, I shook hands with her. "Nice to meet you, Ava."

"You too! I can guarantee you that we're going to have so much fun together. Probably be drinking buddies, too." She gave me a wink and tapped me on the shoulder.

"Oh, can I join?" Caleb stepped into the conversation.

"You can wish," Ava replied with a smirk.

Caleb made a sad face, then Ava said something else; however, I had already lost interest in the conversation when I noticed someone else eying us. He moved his eyes quickly and concentrated his gaze on a file that was in his hands when he noticed that I was looking at him.

He was sitting at one of the corner desks and seemed to be in his late twenties or early thirties.

His deep blue eyes were the first thing I noticed about him, and his light-toned face pointed them out exceptionally. He has a stubble beard that made his jawline look even sharper, and his dark brown hair looked a little messy, as if he didn't even bother styling it. And I had to admit, he looked handsome with an appearance that could make him stand out in the crowd. Not like I cared, though.

However, just by looking at him, I could tell that he was the kind of agent who'd been born in a suit—so serious that you couldn't even imagine him as being a baby or infant. They usually spoke in a baritone voice and threw in legalistic words even if we were just having a conversation about the weather. Those kinds of people saw life in no color, either black or white, right or wrong, legal or illegal.

I had to deal with so many of them while I was in Quantico. A little part of me hoped that this wouldn't be the case with this guy, and if it was, I hoped I wouldn't have to work with him on many occasions.

"Alexandra," a familiar voice called from behind me, cutting my thoughts off.

I turned and looked at the source of the voice, putting on a polite smile on my face. "Sir..."

George Wyatt, the assistant special agent in charge of the violent crimes division in New York. He worked with my father and was one of his closest friends and was really close to our family until that day. And he used to visit me when I moved in with my grandparents in the first few months following the incident, but his visits eventually stopped. I was even kind of surprised that he still remembered me.

And just by looking at him, I could see how the years had changed him as well. His hair was all grey now except for a few black hairs here and there. And the wrinkles around his dark brown eyes were a sign of the many years of experience he had lived and all the things he had seen while he was still a field agent.

"I felt so glad when I heard that you were joining our team today." He gave me a kind smile. "Your father would have been very proud."

"Thank you, sir," I said, giving him a little smile of my own.

"You're going to be assigned to your first case soon. In the meantime, I would like to see you in my office," he told me, and I nodded. While he was walking upstairs to his office, he called on one of the other agents. "Hunt, see me at my office."

I watched as that said agent rose from his seat, and he was no one but the same man I had caught earlier eying us. He gave me a look that I felt was cold, and it made me a little unnerved. Then he started walking up the stairs behind Wyatt, without looking in my direction again.

My eyebrows knitted into a frown as I focused my gaze on him until he disappeared inside the office, then I sighed and followed the both of them.

I made it to the office. Wyatt was sitting behind his large desk and motioned for me to sit on the chair opposite his desk, next to that agent. I sat and waited impatiently to hear whatever Wyatt had planned for both of us.

"Hunt, you don't have a partner, do you?" Wyatt started, addressing the callous agent.

"No, sir. I don't," Agent Hunt answered in a preserved, calm tone. Although, I could see that he was a little high-strung.

"Well, you do now," Wyatt stated. "From now on, Agent Ryan is going to be your partner."

I blinked. So much for not working with him on many occasions. Deep down, I really had a feeling that this wasn't going to turn out well.

"With all due respect, sir. I prefer working alone," Hunt argued between gritted teeth. "I don't need a partner."

I gave him a death glare that he didn't see because he was keeping his eyes fixed on Wyatt.

"Well, it's a good thing that I'm not asking for your opinion," Wyatt dismissed and then looked between the both of us. "You are going to be assigned to your first case together soon. End of discussion."

Agent Hunt, who looked fuming, excused himself before storming out of the office. I blinked a few times before I excused myself too and decided to go find him.

"Hey, wait," I called after him.

He stopped in his footsteps and turned around, his eyes shooting daggers at me. "What do you want?" he yelled at me.

What a jackass!

"Seriously, what's wrong with you?" I asked, moving my hands in frustration.

He narrowed his eyes at me. "Look, I don't work with partners, and yet I have the highest rank of case closure. Now, I have to babysit you."

It took me a moment to process what he had just said. I twitched up an eyebrow. "Excuse me?"

"I saw the way Wyatt was talking to you. You seem to be his relative or something, and maybe that's also the reason behind how you ended up working here," he spat. "He must have assigned you to be my partner so I can protect you. But sorry, I'm not a babysitter."

Clenching my fist, I tried to calm myself down as much as possible because hitting his pretty damn face was very tempting at the moment. "I don't know who you think you are, and I don't even care about your stupid rate of case closure. But you don't get to talk to me this way or underestimate me or my abilities when you know nothing about me," I snapped. "And for your information, I was at the top of my class at the FBI Academy in Quantico, and I'm the one who chose this place when I had the opportunity to go to DC. And Wyatt was a friend of my father who I haven't seen in almost a decade and a half. Oh, and I don't need your stupid protection because I'm very capable of protecting my own self."

He had wide eyes, and I was breathing heavily. He tried to open his mouth, but I didn't give him a chance. "By the way, you should try humility. I hear that it's pretty good for the soul. And you might also want to try getting over yourself, jerk." I didn't wait for his response and walked away.

Now, I was really looking forward to our first case together as I was more than determined to prove myself in front of that asshole and show him what I was really capable of...

Chapter 2

I went and sat at the desk that was given to me in the open bullpen, and I almost believed that there was smoke coming out of my ears, just like in cartoons. I groaned; I really should have kicked him where it hurt the most and the sun never shone.

"Hey, I heard you and Hunt got assigned together." Ava's voice cut my thoughts off. "Rumors transfer fast around here," she explained when she noticed that my eyebrows were tangled in a confused frown.

I sighed. "Yeah, but apparently, he isn't very enthusiastic about it." Understatement of the year.

She chuckled. "He's actually one of the best agents around here, so I guess the idea of having a partner might have hurt his ego."

I was about to retort, but I clasped my lips shut when I noticed Hunt approaching us.

He stopped at my desk and looked at me with a blank face. "We just received our first case. We need to leave. Now." He gave me his back the second the last word left his mouth and started walking toward the elevator.

My eyes squinted at his attitude, but he didn't see me. Ava sent me a smile that I sensed was both apologetic and supportive. I sighed before I stood up and followed Hunt.

"We will take my car," he said once I joined him in the elevator.

Something inside of me snapped. "Listen, you don't get to treat me that way or order me around by any means. We're partners; you're not my boss."

He narrowed his eyes at me. "I'm not giving you an order, but can you think about it for a second? Why the hell are we going to use two cars when we are going to the same destination?"

Well, he had a point, but I rolled my eyes at him, anyway. I decided to walk silently next to him until we reached his car, which was a Ford Explorer. We both got in and he started driving toward the crime scene.

The drive was full of awkward silence until I finally decided to break it after I realized that he hadn't even briefed me about the case. "So, what's this case about?"

"It's a homicide," he answered coldly, maintaining his gaze on the road.

"Oh, thank you. I have no idea what I'd have done without your super helpful enlightenment." I rolled my eyes, sarcasm dripping off my tone.

He fixed me with a hard glare. "Oh, look at that; I think you have a good sense of humor."

"At least one of us does." I gave him a side look, wanting to get on his nerves.

I swear I could see him smile a little, but he covered it quickly. "A woman in her late-thirties was murdered in her house. One neighbor discovered the body and called the police and they asked for our help due to the heinous nature of the crime."

I nodded before turning to look at him. I sighed. "Look, we have to work together whether we like it or not. The least we can do is act like we tolerate each other. Is that okay with you, Agent Hunt?"

"Liam," he muttered, still focusing his eyes on the road.

"What?" I raised an eyebrow.

"My name is Liam," he said, looking at me. "We're going to be stuck with each other for a while, and it's better if we're on a first-name basis, Alexandra."

I smiled a little. "In that case, please call me Alex." I always preferred people around me to call me Alex instead of Alexandra.

"Alright, Alex," he said with the slightest of smiles before he returned his gaze to the road.

"Are you naturally this much of a pain, or do you try?" I turned to look at him with a smirk.

He looked at me with a raised eyebrow. "And aren't you just full of sarcasm?"

"Oh, I know. Isn't it great?" I shrugged with a grin. "It's one of the many perks of being in my company."

He narrowed his eyes at me but said nothing. I laughed under my breath and decided to take pity on him. I concentrated my gaze out the window for the rest of the ride.

A while later, we reached a suburban neighborhood on the Upper East Side. Liam gestured to one of the houses. "That's our house."

He put the car in park, and we both got out and headed toward the house. Two officers were standing in front of it; we showed them our badges and they let us in.

"Agent Hunt, good to have you here," one of the police officers said as he shook hands with Liam.

"Officer Jones, this is Agent Ryan," Liam said, looking at me. He threw me a look before he continued. "My partner."

I narrowed my eyes at him before I shook hands with the officer. After that, Officer Jones led us to the living room where the body was found.

A woman was lying on the floor with her eyes wide open and a pool of her own blood surrounding her.

My eyes immediately traveled to the wounds on her head—the ones that ended her life. I had to admit that the scene was gruesome. Someone had struck this poor woman with a hard object on her head with extreme force more than once. Her skull was broken, and small parts of her brain had fallen out of it and were lying on the floor next to her.

Swallowing hard, I pushed down the lump that had formed in my throat.

"Alisson Clark; thirty-nine. Judging by the stiffness of the body, the expected time of death is between 8 and 10 AM," Officer Jones began. "One of her neighbors came to check on her saying that she heard loud screams. She found the door wide open, so she went inside and found the body. Also, we have looked everywhere, but the murder weapon was nowhere to be found here or in the surrounding area."

I wouldn't lie. I felt a little uneasy; this was my first case, after all. Liam put on a pair of gloves before stepping in to examine the body. I took a deep breath before I did the same.

"What's the cause of death?" Liam asked.

I stepped more forward. "Judging by the injuries on her head, it's probably a severe fracture to the base of the skull that damaged the tissues of the brain due to blunt force trauma, causing instant death. Or she may have lost her consciousness and died from bleeding out after a short time. Well, the autopsy results will reveal that after all," I said, looking at the body thoroughly. However, my money was on the former because the trauma to the head was pretty ugly. Blood and brains were splattered across the floor. "But there are over six different injuries. The culprit had to hit her more than once to make sure she was dead. I think some of the blows were even inflicted post-mortem."

Liam looked at me with a raised eyebrow for a few seconds before he added. "There are no signs of struggle visible on her, but yes, we have to wait for the autopsy results to make sure."

"But this could mean that she knew her killer," I suggested. "I don't believe that this might be something like a burglary that went wrong."

"Was there anything missing from the house?" Liam asked the detective.

"We don't know yet," Officer Jones answered. "There are no signs of breaking and entering, and there's no mess anywhere in the house. Anyway, we are waiting for the husband to confirm that."

"Did someone call him?" I asked, referring to the victim's husband.

"Yeah, he's on his way here," Officer Jones replied.

Liam rose to his feet. "Agent Ryan and I will look through the house until he arrives."

I rose to my feet and looked at him. "Where to start?"

"Let's start with the main bedroom," he replied, and I nodded in agreement.

We went to the bedroom and started looking every-where for something unusual, but everything was in place, and nothing seemed out of the ordinary. I started searching the nightstands and my hands fell on some medications.

"Are those sleeping pills?" Liam asked, pointing at the bottles in my hand.

"No, I think they're meant to be taken after abortions or miscarriages," I answered, then I met Liam's gaze. "She had recently lost a baby."

He nodded before letting out a huff. "I found nothing."

I was about to say me too, but we heard loud voices coming from downstairs, so we went to check out what was happening.

"No, Alisson. She can't be gone!" a man shouted in disbelief.

"This is the husband," Officer Jones whispered to us.

"Mr. Clark, I'm Agent Hunt, and this is Agent Ryan. We're with the FBI," Liam introduced us. "I'm terribly sorry for your loss, but you have to cooperate with us, so we can find whoever did that to your wife."

Mr. Clark nodded slowly; signs of shock were still visible on him.

"We would like you to check if anything is missing from the house, but you can do that later. First, we need to ask you some questions," Liam started. "Did your wife have any kind of foes or someone who would want to hurt her?"

"No, Alisson was kind to everyone. I can't think of anyone who would want to do that to her," Mr. Clark answered, his voice breaking a little.

"Okay, can you please tell me your whereabouts today between 8 and 10 AM?"

"Why?" Mr. Clark asked, his tone rising. "Do you think that I might have done that to her?"

"It's not like that, sir. We just want to make sure of everything and put our records straight," I said, trying to reassure him.

The man looked between the both of us and sighed. "I left the house at 7 and arrived at work at 8 AM. I didn't leave un—until they called and told me about what happened to Alisson." His voice broke again. "You can check with my co-workers."

Liam ordered someone to check if that was true.

"Sir, could you tell me about your wife's mental health after losing the baby?" I asked. "Were there any changes in her routine or attitude?" I thought that maybe the loss of her baby triggered her to do something impulsive that might have gained her enemies.

I watched as Mr. Clark's face fell. "What baby?" he questioned, giving me a bewildered look.

I swallowed hard, sensing that things would soon take an even more drastic turn. "Sir, did you know if your wife was on any medications?"

The man shook his head. Liam and I shared a nervous look.

"Mr. Clark, we found some medications in your room. We believe it belonged to your wife," Liam explained, sounding a little uneasy. "It's used after abortions or miscarriages."

The man narrowed his eyes to a squint and started talking between gritted teeth. "Alisson and I kept trying so hard to get pregnant for almost ten years. We didn't check with any doctors. I didn't want her to feel bad if she was the infertile one, so I examined myself without telling her." He paused for a moment. "And I found out that I was sterile, but I hadn't had enough courage to tell her."

My eyes widened as the realization hit me, but I covered it quickly.

I noticed a vein popping on Mr. Clark's neck, and his tone increased as he continued to talk. "So, you can't be telling me that my wife was pregnant, as this can't be possible. Alisson couldn't have had a baby unless—" He paused, as if he was trying to grasp the idea, then he shook his head before looking at us with eyes full of both doubt and agony. "There must be a mistake because if it's true, it would mean..." He looked between me and Liam in disbelief. "No, Alisson would never cheat on me." Tears were gathering in his eyes as he finished.

"Sir, it's possible that there might be some kind of misunderstanding. We need to wait for the medical examiner's report to make sure," I said, trying to give him some reassurance.

The man nodded, but I could see that his eyes were still full of doubt.

"While we wait, could you tell us about the people who were close to your wife? Any close friends or relatives with whom she might have kept secrets?" Liam asked, getting a notebook and a pen out of his pocket.

"Yeah, her best friend's name is Audrey Matthews, but she's currently out of the state," the man said in disappointment, but then he seemed as if he remembered something. "She used to keep a diary; it's in our room. I never looked inside of it as I knew it was very private to her, but now I think that I really should have done that." He scoffed at the last part.

"That's really helpful, sir," I told him. "Maybe you could wait here with the officers and try to look around the house to check if there's anything unusual or missing, and we will let you know if we find anything."

Mr. Clark nodded and walked away with some officers.

"That was quite awkward," Liam said, letting out a sigh.

"Tell me about it." I sighed, shaking my head.

"Now let's go find that journal and dig into Mrs. Clark's mysterious, and apparently, very eventful life." He started walking up the stairs toward the bedroom and I followed him.

We searched the room all over again, but we were having a hard time finding the diary. I decided to look through her wardrobe again, more thoroughly this time.

"I found it!" I exclaimed once I found hidden inside a secret drawer that was behind some of her clothes.

"Okay, let's see if it has anything useful," Liam said.

Opening the journal, I started scanning through it in a quick pattern. I stopped when I reached some pages that were written almost three months ago.

"Well, it looks like we won't need to wait for the medical examiner's report, after all," I said before I handed the journal to Liam.

"Wow, that's pretty detailed," Liam said, his blue eyes widening a little as he looked through the journal.

I had to agree with that. "She was writing about someone called Nick."

"Yeah, but no last name, though," Liam said in disappointment as he closed the journal.

"Yeah." I sighed. "But we should ask Mr. Clark if he knows any Nicks."

Liam nodded. "I really pity that man. This's a lot to grasp."

I nodded. I couldn't agree more. Receiving two blows in the head at once got to hurt pretty badly, for sure.

We went downstairs and informed Mr. Clark about what we found. To say that the man was hurt was an understatement, and I was really feeling sorry for him. He went through so many agonies of a lifetime in only a few hours.

However, when we asked him about knowing anybody with the name Nick, all that hurt turned into fury, and he seemed like he was ready to kill someone.

"That son of a bitch!" he barked, walking back and forth, fuming.

"Sir, do you know who that is?" I asked in measured tones.

"He is my best friend. The fucking bastard is my best friend." Mr. Clark scoffed, a vein popping on his neck. "Three months ago, I had to travel outside of the country for work and I asked him to take care of my wife while I was gone." He laughed bitterly. "Well, he definitely took care of her, after all."

"Mr. Clark, do you know where he lives?" Liam asked.

"Yes," Mr. Clark answered with clenched teeth.

"Good, because I believe we have to pay him a visit," Liam decided, sharing a look with me...

Chapter 3

"**O**kay, got it. Thank you, Doctor," Liam said through the phone before he hung up and turned to look at me. "That was the medical e x a m i n - er."

"And what does he have to say?" I asked, pushing him to continue.

"Well, she indeed had a miscarriage only a few weeks ago," he replied. "Our murder weapon was definitely a hard object. They say the first blow was the fatal one. It caused severe brain lacerations and hemorrhage, just like you suggested earlier. The unsub inflicted the rest of the injuries postmortem."

I watched as he had made a face as if it had bothered him to admit that I was right. I rolled my eyes at his reaction. "Was there anything else?"

"Well, apparently our guy took his sweet time cleaning the scene, as there were no fingerprints found anywhere. However, they found debris of a blue fabric under her nails, which they believe belongs to the unsub. Unfortunately, no DNA was found, though," he said while maintaining his gaze on the road.

I nodded, even though I wasn't sure he saw me. I moved my head to focus on the outside of my window, and it was dead silence for the rest of the ride. Thoughts trundled in my brain like a through train, with no intention of stopping. Thoughts about my first day at the FBI, the case, and whether my partnership with Liam was going to work out or not.

"This is the address that Mr. Clark gave us." Liam's voice finally put that train of thought to a stop.

He parked the car in front of a two-floor house. We both got out of the car and walked toward the house. Liam rang the doorbell. A man who appeared to be in his mid-forties opened the door. His neatly styled hair was a mix of salt and pepper, and he looked between us with dark eyes full of skepticism.

"Mr. Nick Walden?" Liam began.

"Yes?" he answered in measured tones.

We both got our badges and showed them to him. Skepticism was shortly replaced with an expression that screamed nervousness.

"We're with the FBI. We would like to ask you a few questions," Liam told him.

He looked at us with eyes clouded with evident stress and worry for a few moments before he sighed and gestured to the inside of the house. We got in, and he led us to the living room.

"Sir, did you happen to hear that Allison Clark was found dead today?" Liam spoke up once we were all seated.

His eyes widened in obvious shock, but he covered it quickly. He swallowed hard before he spoke. "Oh god, h—how did that happen? What about Henry? Is he okay?"

"Yes. Mr. Clark is fine," Liam answered in a calm tone.

"Good." He let out a breath of relief that I could tell was fake. He looked at us with a hint of seriousness in his eyes. "But wait, what does that have to do with me?"

"Sir, we found out about the relationship you had with Mrs. Clark," I spoke for the first time since we got here, not intending to sugarcoat anything. I made sure to keep eye contact with him and watch for his reaction.

He seemed taken aback for a couple of seconds, then his expression turned into pure anger as his face gained a few shades of red. "This is bullshit. I don't know what you are talking about!" he chided while shaking his head.

"Well, did you know she used to keep a diary?" Liam asked in a challenging tone.

The man's eyes widened in realization.

"She aborted your baby a few weeks ago," Liam continued, not giving him the chance to tell any more lies. "We called the clinic where she had the abortion and they told us she wasn't alone. They said that her husband was by her side the whole time, but the description didn't match Mr. Clark—it matches you. Besides, they heard her calling you Nicky."

I held myself from grinning. He was good.

The man turned a few shades paler and started sweating. "I can't believe that she wrote about what we had between us in her stupid diary." He scoffed. "Yes, Alisson and I had an affair. She surprised me with the baby thing, saying that she wanted to keep it and leave Henry so we could be together." He sighed. "But I just couldn't do that. I felt guilty, okay? Henry is my best friend, and I already have a family. I love my wife and my son, and I wasn't willing to give them up at any cost. I was planning to end the relationship as soon as possible and I made sure she knew that, so she decided to have an abortion."

My respect for the man sitting in front of me was decreasing with every word that left his mouth. An honorable man, indeed. I cleared my throat and fixed my gaze on him. "Sir, where were you today between 8 and 10 AM?"

"I was at work. I didn't leave until 5 PM. You can make sure of my alibi there," he answered, crossing his hands as he looked between us in annoyance. "Look, I wanted to end the relationship, but I would never hurt her."

Liam nodded. "During the time you spent with Mrs. Clark, did you notice anything unusual about her behavior, or if she had any enemies or people threatening her?"

The man was about to reply to Liam's question, but he got interrupted by the front door opening, followed by a teenage boy stepping inside. He was wearing a blue baseball jacket and had a baseball kit with him.

"Dad, I'm home—" He stopped in his tracks when he noticed us. "W—What's going on?"

"Nothing that needs your concern," Mr. Walden quickly told him. "Go to your room, Justin."

I could see that the boy's bottom lip was quivering. He was also sweating, and his hands were shaking. I knew that some people usually got edgy with the presence of law enforcement, and he was just a kid after all. But my gut feeling told me that something was off. He concentrated his gaze on Liam and me for a couple of seconds, hazel eyes full of unmasked fear, then he headed upstairs.

Liam and I shared a look, and I knew he was having suspicions as well.

"If you have any other questions, please hurry before my wife arrives," Mr. Walden demanded.

"Mr. Walden, does your son know anything about the affair you had with Mrs. Clark?" Liam asked.

The man's dark eyes filled with fury. "Of course, not. My son has nothing to do with this!"

"Thank you for your time, Mr. Walden," Liam told him. "We're done here for today." He made sure to emphasize the fact that things weren't over. "This's my card. Please call me if you remember anything else."

Liam handed him the card, then we left the house and got inside the car. We sat there idly without bringing the car to life and it was dead silence for a couple of minutes.

"Did you notice what happened in there?" Liam asked. "Something was just too fishy."

"Sadly, I did." I sighed and looked at him. "The kid was wearing a blue jacket and baseball bats can turn into very brutal weapons."

Liam sighed. "He might have known about the relationship and got mad. We need to check him out."

"Our list of suspects keeps getting bigger," I mused. "Walden had a motive, as well as Clark himself. He might've known about his wife's pregnancy earlier than he lets on."

Liam nodded, rubbing his eyes with the palms of his hand. He then looked at me with blue eyes that were worn out from exhaustion. "A few months ago, there was a stalker in town. A young, sick man who used to keep track of middle-aged women who lived in upper-class neighborhoods. He used to break into their houses and steal some of their personal belongings, and that was it. But things eventually went from bad to worse when he started creating fantasies about those women. He hit a breaking point and slaughtered a woman because she was seeing someone, and he thought she was cheating on him. And his violent urges didn't stop there; he also hurt and incapacitated many other women. The case was widely publicized, and it terrorized everyone for a while. Then, we finally managed to catch the guy, and they placed him in a mental institution.

"The M.O. here is very similar. The local PD thought it might be the handiwork of a copycat, and that's why they called us on this case pretty quickly. But I'm starting to doubt that it's anywhere close to that scenario here."

"I read about that case, and I thought it was brilliant work. The guy's profile was dead-on, and you guys set up the perfect ambush to catch him." I fixed my position to face Liam and looked at him with an amused look. "You were the case's agent, weren't you? The whole thing was your idea."

I watched as his eyes lit up with pride, and his lips titled up in a slight smile. It was all the confirmation I needed.

I chuckled, shaking my head. "So you may turn out to be as good as I heard, after all."

"Oh, not really." He shook his head before looking at me with a mischievous smile. "I'm better."

I scoffed, narrowing my eyes at him. "You know what? I take that back."

He let out a small laugh that I felt was genuine, and that was a first, but it only lasted for a little while before he changed the subject. "I think we should really call it a day. What do you think?"

The second those words left his mouth, an involuntary yawn escaped my lips. It was like I didn't realize how exhausted I was until he mentioned it.

Liam grinned. "I guess that's a yes." He inserted his key into the ignition. "Anyway, I have a feeling that another long day is waiting for us tomorrow."

I agreed with all my heart as we finally hit the road.

We first went back to the bureau and asked our technical analysts to look into the kid. After that, we both went home to get our deserved rest...

***

The following morning, I met Liam at the FBI building.

"Justin Walden was seen around Mrs. Clark's neighborhood yesterday," he told me. "We have to go get him from school for questioning. He's currently our prime suspect."

I agreed, even though I was feeling a little sorry for the kid. "We also need to notify his parents. He's still a minor, after all."

He nodded. "We can ask one of our guys to talk to them. Now we need to pick him up from school."

We informed our communication liaisons of the current situation so they would speak with the parents, then Liam and I drove to Justin's high school. We knew that the two of us were more than enough to handle him.

The second we walked into the school, everybody started eying us warily, and I remembered just how much I hated high school.

We went to the principal's office, showed him our badges, and asked to talk with Justin. He informed us that Justin was playing baseball on the school's field and led us there. We found Justin sitting alone on a bench, and—fortunately for us—he was wearing the same blue baseball jacket from yesterday.

We started walking toward him; however, when he noticed that we were approaching him, he panicked and stoop up at once, then he started running. Liam and I wasted no time and started chasing after him.

After a short time of playing cat and mouse, I made it closer to him before I jumped and tackled him to the floor with his hands behind his back.

"Justin Walden, you have the right to remain silent," I said through heavy breaths as I slapped my handcuffs on him. Then I helped him up to his feet and continued reading him the Miranda rights. I could see Liam smirking from afar as I escorted the kid back to the car.

That was indeed a lot for my first case...

***

We took Justin to the FBI building and put him in one of the interrogation rooms.

Watching from the observation room, I noticed that the kid was shaking, sweating, and was only a shade darker than Casper. I figured out that if we waited any longer; he was probably going to have a panic attack.

"Go in," Liam told me. "Try to calm him down a little. His parents just arrived in case he needs them present."

"Aren't you coming in with me?" I raised my eyebrows in question.

"Well, if we both go in, we would have to play good cop, bad cop. And I really think that's the last thing this kid needs right now," he replied with a shrug. "Besides, it will be your first real interrogation. I think you should do it solo." He looked at me with a slight smirk.

I gave him a little smile before I straightened my expression and took a deep breath before opening the door to the interrogation room.

Justin jumped the second I walked inside, and he looked startled. I closed the door behind me, and the sound echoed through the room. His worried eyes followed me until I sat on the chair opposite him.

"I did nothing wrong," he began, fidgeting a little in his seat.

"Well, if that's true, why did you run from us and resisted arrest?"

He didn't answer me and just swallowed hard.

"Justin, do you understand your rights?" I asked, keeping my eyes on him. "You can refuse to be questioned without a lawyer present. Also, as a minor, you can have your parents with you during the interview."

"No." The boy shook his head almost immediately. "I don't want them here."

"Okay." I nodded. "Let's start with something easy. What were you doing in the Manhattan Valley neighborhood yesterday?"

His eyes widened, and he turned even paler. "I—I was visiting a friend." His hand rose to touch his face—a sign that he was lying.

"Was that friend Allison Clark, by any chance?" I gave him a challenging look, making sure he knew his lies were pointless.

I could see that he was panicking, and the tremors in his hands increased. He clutched them tightly.

I stood up and walked to a corner table that had a few items on top of it. I poured a glass of water, and then I handed it to Justin. "Here, drink this."

He took it from me and was having a hard time trying not to spill it all over him.

I waited until he started looking a little calmer, then I tried again. "Justin, I know that you're aware of the relationship your father had with Mrs. Clark." I pushed his buttons even more. "Some neighbors saw a teenage boy with a blue jacket and a baseball kit on his shoulder hanging around the neighborhood. I believe that matches your description."

He said nothing and continued to rub his hands while avoiding eye contact with me.

I sighed. "Listen, there's no law against hanging around in neighborhoods. Just tell me why you were there."

He looked at me for a second before running his shaky hands through his hair. He swallowed hard, then his lips slowly parted, and he finally spoke. "I—I went to talk to her."

I didn't comment as I waited for him to continue.

"I read her messages to my father. I ignored it at first, so Mom wouldn't know. But then my parents started to fight, and I knew it was because of that woman, so I—I went to ask her to leave my father."

"You know that she was murdered, right?" I waited for a reaction or for him to say something, but he didn't, so I continued. "She was hit on her head with something hard, like a baseball bat. And forensics found some blue fabrics under her nails."

He looked at me in fear, and his lips trembled. And I watched as his hands traveled to his blue jacket, adjusting it as if it chafed him all of a sudden.

I didn't stop. "The forensic team is currently running a luminol blood test on your baseball bats as we speak to see if any of them have blood remains. And we will examine your jacket later for a fabric match."

I was still trying to push his limits, but I might have already hit his breaking point.

A loud sob escaped his mouth. "I didn't mean it," he whispered so quietly I could barely hear him.

I kept my eyes fixed on him but said nothing, knowing for sure that he would continue.

"When I went there, I begged her to walk away from my father. She held me by my collar and mocked me, saying that I was just a kid who understood nothing. Then she insulted my mother; she said that my father hated her and didn't want her anymore." Hatred was obvious in his words as he spat them. "I became so angry that I didn't know what I was doing until I had already hit her with my baseball bat. She collapsed to the floor, and she looked like she was already gone, but I didn't stop. It was like I have lost all control over myself. I kept hitting and hitting until I was no longer able to."

Tears started dripping from his eyes like showers. I kept watching him without saying anything.

"I felt relieved for a couple of minutes. But after that, I returned to reality, and I couldn't believe what I had done, so I ran. I didn't even have the guts to throw the baseball bat away," he admitted. "I had no intention of doing something like that; I didn't want to hurt her. All I wanted was to get her away from my father. I never wanted to kill her. Never, I swear."

He completely broke down in tears. "I'm sorry. I'm so sorry."

At this moment, I should have been happy that I got a full confession out of him, and that I just closed my first case, but I wasn't. I kept watching him, all guilty and full of regret, as he kept apologizing, over and over again.

People said that a guilty conscience needed no accuser. Once you felt guilty about something, it would keep haunting you forever. It would shackle you; it would suffocate and smother you until you confess or make things right.

And that was why I always believed that a clear conscience was the most powerful punishment a guilty person could ever have.

Chapter 4

I watched as two agents escorted a crying, handcuffed Justin outside of the interrogation room.

"It's second-degree murder," Liam said when I stepped out of the interrogation room. "I doubt they'll treat him as a minor in court. He'll probably be sent to an adult's prison."

"I know."

Letting out a sigh, I couldn't help but feel a little sorry for him. The kid wanted to prevent the destruction of his family and ended up committing murder.

"That was great for a first case, wasn't it?" He gave out a little sarcastic laugh before he looked at me. "Welcome to the FBI, Alex."

I worked in the violent crimes unit, so I didn't really expect anything less, yet it was still overwhelming. Anyway, I decided to change the subject. "Now tell me, do we get to have coffee breaks or not?" I was dying for a caffeine fix and preferably something other than the office coffee that tasted like mud. After all, there wasn't a thing a good cup of coffee couldn't fix.

"We do," he answered with a slight smile. "I also happen to know a place we can go to."

***

There were lots of coffee shops in the area, but Liam chose one in particular. He said it was the best, and I took his word on it.

We walked into the coffee shop and the pleasant smell of brewing coffee and freshly baked muffins immediately welcomed us. It was like a warm hug after a long, hard day.

The royal blue and white colors of the walls and the tables glistened in the golden rays of the sunshine. We ordered our coffees and paid for them before we chose a table that was a little far away from the fuss.

My eyes started wandering around the coffee shop. A few people were having an amicable conversation as they sipped on their coffees. Others had their eyes fixed on their laptops as they tried to finish some of their loaded work. Some people were enjoying their coffees with a book in their hands, being engulfed in a whole unique world of their own. And there were a few students who had pencils in their hands. Some of them were typing down on their notebooks while others seemed in deep thought—probably trying to solve a complex mathematical equation. I felt that this place was always full of people so close, yet so apart.

As human beings, we always needed the sense of others, even if we were alone. And I thought that this kind of atmosphere made all these people somehow feel like they belonged to a tribe, even if they didn't know it.

Feeling the tenseness leaving my shoulders, I smiled in satisfaction and took a long sip of my coffee. "You were right. This's great."

"I tried most of the coffee shops around here, but this was the best so far." He smiled, looking pleased with himself. He took a large sip of his own cup before he looked at me again. "You did a great job working up your first case, and that actually brings me to the little argument we had yesterday."

I gave him my full concentration, waiting for what he had to say about that.

"I'm sorry for what I said, and for judging and underestimating you when I barely knew anything about you," he said, maintaining his eyes on me, which I could tell were full of genuine regret.

I gave him a slight smile. "Apology accepted. But was it too hard, though?" I raised my eyebrow at him, and I saw him giving me a sly smirk. "Anyway, I'm sorry too, for calling you a jerk and an asshole."

"I don't remember you calling me an asshole." He looked at me with a raised eyebrow.

I smirked. "Oh, I did in my head. Alongside so many other insults."

He chuckled and took a large sip of his coffee, but added nothing else.

I refused to allow silence to take place and wanted to keep the conversation alive, so I asked him a question that I really wanted to know the answer to. "So, why do you really hate working with partners?"

I noticed that his face and eyes dropped a fraction, but he covered that change quickly and looked at me with his usual expression—a poker face. "Because they can be a burden and they can really slow you down." His tone was sarcastic, and he plastered half a smile on his face.

I felt that there was a lot more to that subject, but I had a feeling that he didn't feel comfortable about sharing, so I decided to let it drop and lighten up the mood a little. "Oh, I totally see where you're coming from, and I hope you won't be a burden to me."

"I'll try my best." He let out a soft laugh. He took a sip of his coffee while keeping his gaze on me. "So, why exactly did you choose here over DC?"

"You're new to New York, aren't you?" I smiled as I put my elbow on the table and rested my face on my palm.

I felt that my question took him by surprise.

He cleared his throat and looked at me. "I don't see why this's relevant to the question I just asked you."

"Because for us, true New Yorkers, no place else is good enough." I gave him a smug look. I really loved New York, but it wasn't the full truth, though. My father had worked in New York's violent crimes unit for years, and that was mainly why I decided to work there. He was always the one I looked up to, and I really hoped that he had somehow come to know that I had fulfilled my dream and was trying so hard to fit in his shoe.

I was never that spiritual, and sometimes, I found it hard to believe when people told me that my parents were watching over me every step of the way. Because all I could remember was the feeling of loneliness I had to live with all my life.

However, sometimes, that thought succeeded in bringing me some peace. The idea that they were really there, watching me from the other side. That they had seen me in my prom dress and when I was valedictorian. That they were there at my graduation ceremony when I finally received my FBI badge and were there to bring me warmth whenever I was feeling like the worst version of myself.

"Hey, you okay?"

Liam's voice brought me back into the real world. I nodded, putting on a fake smile and a strong façade. "Yeah, I just got a little distracted." I knew he had noticed my change of expression, but I was relieved when he decided to not point it out.

He nodded and smiled. "Anyway, you're actually right. I'm originally from Seattle. I worked in the field office there for a while before I moved here."

I grinned in triumph before I threw in another question. "So, why did you decide to move to New York?"

"Well, they say people always come to New York to be born again." He shrugged, giving me a vague answer.

I see, two could play that game. I knew that trust didn't come overnight and that we would need some time to open up to each other.

There was silence for a few minutes. We were drinking whatever was left of our coffees. Liam was the first one to break the silence. "So, um... you said Wyatt and your father were friends?"

"Yeah," I answered. "They have worked together in the past." I was feeling a little uncomfortable that this subject was brought up, but I tried my best not to let it show.

"Worked together?" Liam questioned with a raised eyebrow.

"Yeah." I cleared my throat and let out a deep breath. "My father was an FBI agent, too."

"Oh, really? I didn't know." Liam looked a little surprised. "But you said was. Did he retire or something?"

"No," I answered with uneasiness while drawing circles on the top of the cup with my finger. I avoided looking him in the eye. "He and my mother died in an accident when I was ten."

I really hated the orphan girl who watched her parents getting murdered pitiful look, so only a few knew the actual story. Also, it happened a long time ago, and I doubted that the younger agents who worked at the bureau knew anything about it.

"I—I'm so sorry, Alex," he muttered, giving me a soft look.

"Thank you." I gave him a small smile.

He returned the smile back, then there was silence again.

My cup was now empty, and awkwardness was filling the atmosphere. "Shouldn't we be back by now?"

He checked his watch before he replied. "Yeah, we probably should get back to the best part of closing a case—the paperwork." He looked at me with a smirk. "It should be fun."

"Yay, I can't wait," I said with fake enthusiasm as I stood up and tossed my empty cup in the trash bin.

We went back to the FBI building where some agents congratulated me for closing my first case and wished me good luck. After that, I went to my desk and was surprised by the amount of paperwork that was on top of it. Well, Liam didn't lie, after all. This would be a lot of fun.

I wrote my report and filled files for hours, and whenever I thought I was close to being finished, another one popped out of nowhere. After what seemed like forever, I finally finished.

Looking around me, I found that the office was nearly empty as half of the agents had already left for their homes.

Letting out a sigh, I stood up from my chair and stretched my body before I grabbed my blazer and started walking toward the elevator. I checked Liam's desk on my way; it was empty. I took it that he had gone home already.

I made my way to the elevator and clicked on the ground floor button. The door was about to close, but someone stepped inside before it did.

"Oh, Alexandra. Hey." Wyatt smiled at me when he found me inside the elevator.

"Sir." I nodded at him with a polite smile.

"I heard you did a great job on your first case." He gave me a warm smile. "Congratulations."

"Thank you."

"James would have been really proud of you on a day like this."

I was taken aback by what he said, but the sound of the elevator door being opened brought me back to reality. I thanked him with another polite smile before I stepped out of the elevator quickly.

When I got into my car, I started thinking about what Wyatt said. If my father were still alive, would he have approved of me being an FBI agent? Or would he have tried to protect me from all the dangers this job came with? The dangers that he knew so well because they had gotten him killed.

But I remembered what my dad always told me. He used to say that we should always fight for what we believed in and that we should never let ourselves be the puppets of fear.

Letting out a deep breath, I turned the key and brought my car to life.

If I was only sure of just one thing, it was that I believed in what I did. The choice of being an FBI agent was all mine. And I was proud of how it turned out to be...

Chapter 5

Fear. It's a knife in the gut, slowly twisted. A constant hammer on the head. And the shackles keeping me prisoner...

Screams. They made me feel as if my eardrums were going to burst. They told the pain within and made agony seep into my skin.

Blood. Fountains of red filled my nostrils with a sickening metallic smell.

Death. Maybe I had died too along with them, but they just forgot to bury me...

My eyes abruptly shot open. My heart was pounding, and I was panting and covered in sweat.

Inhaling deeply, I tried to calm myself down.

Bloody images flashed through my head when I closed my eyes, forcing me to open them back in an instant. I sighed as I lowered my body back on the bed and stared at the ceiling.

Something was definitely wrong with me.

I was used to having nightmares like the one I had just experienced from time to time. But they have been haunting me nonstop since I started working for the FBI. I couldn't even remember the last time I had a decent night's sleep without waking up in the middle of the night, feeling as if someone had been suffocating me in my sleep.

Grumbling, I kept tossing and turning in bed till the sheets under me became crumpled and wrinkled, as if someone fought a battle on top of them.

I avoided looking at the alarm on my nightstand because it would only prove the fact that I was hardly getting any sleep. Reluctantly, I stole a peek at it and found out that I had almost five hours before having to go to work.

Covering my face with the pillow, I tried to stop my mind from thinking about all the horrible things that have occupied it as if it were a country that had just lost a war. It turned out to be futile, and my mind kept drifting into dreary places.

Throwing the covers away, I got out of bed and went to the kitchen. I pulled out a package of coffee grounds from one of the drawers and added it to the filter before I turned on the coffee machine.

Taking a seat at the kitchen table, I started massaging my tense shoulders to kill time while waiting for my coffee to brew.

I slightly grinned when I heard the heavenly sound of the machine, which meant my precious coffee was ready.

After pouring myself a large cup, I returned to my seat and stared at the freshly made cup of coffee in front of me, steam rising from it. I took it in my hands to steal the heat, feeling pleased with the warmth that transferred to my body. I watched the swirling hues of the coffee that were a blessing as every shade of brown I adored blended so perfectly.

After I took a long sip, my eyes wandered around the empty apartment.

Loneliness never scared me. I was used to it, after all. Most of the time, I even found peace and solace in it. But the more I thought about it, the more I realized that even though I liked being alone, I didn't fancy being alone.

Maybe I should really consider getting a dog.

I let out a long sigh, and then my mind went back to my recurring nightmares. I read once that our brains were hard-wired to remember the bad events in our lives better than the good ones, and I found that pretty ironic. It made me somehow blame our natural biology for my current suffering.

But yet again, I knew that those were memories you could never come close to forgetting, no matter how hard you tried. There was no black box in your brain that could contain them. All you could do was adapt and learn how to live with them.

And I really thought that I had learned how to do that and that the pain had become less with time, but it turned out that I was hugely mistaken.

Remembering the details of that night still brought me so much agony. Like if someone were cutting my insides with shards of glass.

The thoughts accelerated inside my head, and I hoped they would slow down a bit because I was finding it harder to breathe with every second passing.

My heart was hammering in my chest, and my hands were trembling nonstop. I rose from my seat slowly so I wouldn't lose my footing and walked toward the nearest window. I breathed in and out in a slow pattern, trying to calm myself down a little.

It took me a few minutes to regain my normal rhythm of breathing, yet I was still shaking.

Moments like these made me feel the worst. I felt so fragile, and I hated that. It was like being claustrophobic, but in this case, the cage I was trapped in was just my memories.

Sometimes, I used to wonder if I had what it took to be an FBI agent. And thinking about it now, I believed that this sort of thinking somehow had something to do with the nightmares.

Maybe it was too much for me to handle. The job was a constant reminder of what I had lost because my father was an FBI agent too…

Sighing, I looked out the window and noticed that the darkness had started to surrender to the light. The sun rose, filling the sky of New York with brilliant shades of orange. I allowed myself to get lost for a while in this silent beauty.

After the streets of Manhattan were totally illuminated, I decided to go jogging for a while, taking it as a way of distraction.

I ran for a while, then I returned to my apartment and treated myself to a nice shower. After that, I started getting ready for work.

I figured out that I would need a lot of caffeine today, so I stopped by the coffee shop Liam had taken me to.

The barista gave me a warm smile and started preparing my usual order before I even reached the counter. I decided to grab a cup of coffee for Liam too, thinking that it would be a friendly gesture. Besides, he was the one who introduced me to this coffee shop, after all.

Ten minutes later, I made it to the FBI building and up to the floor of the violent crimes unit. I found Liam already sitting at his desk—he was always such an early bird.

Walking toward him, I placed the cup of coffee on his desk without uttering a word.

He looked at the cup of coffee first, then at me. Then, the corners of his mouth lifted up into a smile. "Look at you, being so generous."

"Well, I'm usually a really nice person. Just don't get on my bad side again," I teased, smirking slightly. "Besides, I give you credit for taking me to that coffee shop." I shrugged playfully.

He took a long sip of his coffee before he mumbled. "Well, thank you." He smiled. "And I will make sure to always be in your good graces if that guarantees me a cup of coffee every day."

I rolled my eyes. "Oh, don't count on it." Then I looked at him and tried to hide the desperate look in my eyes. "Anything new?" I was hoping for something to occupy my mind and keep me from overthinking.

"Yup," he answered, handing me a copy of a file. "This case just landed on my desk."

Opening the file, I started reading through it. It wasn't a murder case, but it could be soon. A man had received lots of murder threats, and his wife called the FBI to check them out.

"Alan Miller..." I said, running the name through my head. I thought it was familiar from somewhere.

"He's a famous philanthropist, and that makes him a high-profile target." Liam filled in the blanks in my head.

No wonder why we were handling the case.

"We're taking that threat very seriously."

I nodded as I looked through the rest of the file quickly before I closed it and turned to Liam. "When do we leave?"

"Now," he replied, standing up, then he took his keys off the desk and put his suit jacket on.

I walked next to him, trying to kick all the thoughts that weren't related to the case out of my head.

***

We arrived at Mr. Miller's house. The middle-aged man gave the impression of being decent and amiable. I wondered why someone would want to hurt him.

"So, Mr. Miller. Can you inform us more about these letters?" Liam began, pointing to the letters that were sent to Alan Miller by an anonymous menace. "Maybe you can start off with when you first received them."

I inspected the letters. Unfortunately, they were typed on a computer and then printed, so we wouldn't be able to do handwriting analysis. Also, they seemed to be full of rage and pure hatred, which made me think that whoever sent them knew Mr. Miller personally and was affected by him somehow.

"I have told you before that this's unnecessary," Mr. Miller replied, grabbing my attention. "It's probably someone who wants to have a little fun."

He was about to continue but was cut off by his wife, who had walked into the room. "Whoever is behind this sent those letters to us a week ago when Alan announced the date of the upcoming auction. It's the same date that they threatened to kill Alan on."

"Amanda, you're just overreacting," Mr. Miller tried to argue with his wife.

"Alan, this is your life we're talking about. I'm not taking any chances," she argued, waving her hands in frustration.

"Sir, Mrs. Miller is right. We must take these threats seriously," I said, interrupting both of them. "So, can you tell us about that auction, please?"

The man sighed. "It's one that I have been planning on for years. It's a charity fundraising auction."

"Sir, is there any chance that you could cancel that auction?" Liam asked.

"No!" the man answered almost immediately. "All the money will go to help the people who are suffering and dying out of starvation in Africa's famine. I will never cancel it at any cost—a lot of lives are depending on it."

"Sir, we understand, but—" I was about to say something, but Mr. Miller's phone started ringing and interrupted me.

Mr. Miller sent me an apologetic look before putting the phone to his ear. "Alan Miller," he answered the call.

We all watched as his eyes widened, and he looked at us with eyes clouded with fear.

He covered the phone with his hand and whispered. "I—It's him..."

Chapter 6

"**I**—It's him," Mr. Miller whispered with wide eyes full of fear.

We were expecting something like that to happen, so we had a team of technical analysts with us who started working on their computers immediately after hearing Mr. Miller's words.

"Sir, I need you to talk to him and try to stall him as much as you can," I whispered to Mr. Miller, who was holding the phone with shaky hands.

He nodded before he put the phone back to his ear. "W—Who are you? And why are you doing this?" he asked, his tone a little shaky.

Liam and I put on pairs of headphones so we could hear what the person on the other line had to say.

He was silent for a couple of seconds, but then we heard a growl followed by a voice laced with anger. "Who am I? That doesn't matter. But why? That's because you and your stupid auction destroyed my life."

"I don't understand what you mean," Mr. Miller told him through the phone, frowning. He was clearly oblivious to what the man was talking about.

The man on the other side of the phone gave out a quiet sob before he continued, his voice breaking. "I—It killed her."

Liam and I shared a look.

Mr. Miller had an expression of both shock and confusion, but he said nothing.

"You will pay for what you have done and caused," the man spat his words before he hung up the phone.

"Did you locate him?" Liam asked one of the analysts.

He shrugged, a disappointed look written all over his face. "He was using a burner phone. We couldn't locate him."

Liam groaned. I sighed before I turned to Mr. Miller, who was still in shock. I had to call his name twice before he finally noticed and met my gaze.

"Sir, do you have any idea what that man was talking about?" I asked.

"I—I'm not sure, but..." he started. Then he took a deep breath before he continued. "My assistant died when we were in Africa."

Liam was still talking to the analyst, but what Mr. Miller said had clearly caught his attention.

"How?" he asked.

"It was the first time for her to travel with me," he started to explain. "She caught a contagious disease back there. Her immune system was so weak, and she died because of the infection."

"Was she married?" I asked, and Mr. Miller nodded. "What was her name?" I asked again.

He took a while before answering me. "Dana Stone."

We asked the analysts for information about her husband and the people who were close to her; they came shortly after.

We found out that her husband became an alcoholic after her death and that caused his children to be taken away from him by social services.

Her death was an accident, but it destroyed his life. It was only normal that a man in his situation would try to blame others for all he had lost. So, it made sense that he was seeking revenge, and having the motive to commit an awful crime. And that made him our prime suspect.

Liam and I went to his house alongside some other agents and officers. We knocked on the door a few times, but there was no answer. We had no other choice but to break the door to get in.

We searched the house upside-down but there was no one there.

"What now?" I asked Liam in disappointment, putting my gun back in its holster.

He sighed. "The auction is in two days. We have no choice now but to have it highly secured, and to be there undercover."

Undercover, huh! That was definitely going to be interesting.

***

It was the night of the auction. Mr. Miller refused to let us put any security gates or even search the guests, so we wouldn't scare them off. But we had the building secured from the outside and the inside.

On the outside, both the FBI and SWAT teams were ready to storm in at any second, and on the inside, we had agents undercover everywhere, including me and Liam.

We were attending the auction as normal guests—a couple, actually. Liam was wearing an expensive tuxedo, and I was wearing an elegant black maxi dress, but we still looked so out of place. Talking in our earpieces didn't help our cause at all, either.

I sighed and whispered to Liam. "I think we kind of look inept. This's going to scare him out."

He nodded and walked closer to me, then out of nowhere, he placed his hands on my side, radiating an electric shock that went through my whole body.

His sudden act took me by surprise, and I felt my cheeks burning. I looked at him with frowned eyebrows, but he just shrugged and gave me an innocent look.

His mouth twitched into a half-smile. "Well, the least we could do is try to blend in a little. We're supposed to be a couple, remember?"

I was about to argue with him, but something else caught my attention.

Two men were standing in front of us having a conversation. One of them had a glass of champagne in his hand and a strange tattoo on that same hand. I tried to focus on the tattoo, and when I finally did, my eyes widened in fear, and I felt paralyzed.

It was that same tattoo—the same one that kept haunting me for years.

"Hey, you okay?" Liam asked with a raised eyebrow, his voice bringing me back to reality.

I nodded at him with a slight smile and returned to look at where the man was standing, but my eyes found nothing. He was like a ghost who disappeared into thin air.

Damn it! Was my mind playing tricks on me now and making me imagine things?

I shook my head, trying to clear my head when I watched Mr. Miller walking up to the stage. He tapped the mic and greeted the guests, then he gave a powerful and moving speech about helping people in need. After that, he announced the start of the auction.

We tried to keep our eyes on Mr. Miller the whole time, but the place was full of men in tuxedos, making our task difficult.

Some other agents were supposed to be watching Mr. Miller, but Liam and I were appalled when we heard in our earpieces that they had lost eyes on him.

We looked at each other in fear and asked if any of the other agents had sight of him. The answer was negative, so our fear was now accompanied by panic.

"Damn it!" Liam cursed through the earpiece before he turned to me. "We need to find him."

I nodded. "It's better if we separate."

He nodded, and we went in different ways.

I looked for him everywhere, but he was nowhere to be found. I made it to a corridor that had a few locked rooms, including the bathrooms, and then suddenly, I heard a noise coming out of the men's bathroom.

I took out my gun that was hidden in my clutch, then I carefully opened the door a little to take a peek at the situation.

The attacker was holding a terrified Alan Miller at gunpoint and was repeating things like 'You destroyed my life, and you now have to pay for it.'

I asked for backup before I burst into the room. I pointed my gun at the assailant. "FBI, drop your weapon!" I yelled. I could now see him clearly—he was the deceased assistant's husband.

He looked at me and groaned loudly, keeping his gun pointed in Miller's direction. "I can't. He has to pay for what he had done."

"I have nothing to do with what happened to your wife. Why can't you understand?" Mr. Miller told him with a pleading voice.

"If she didn't have to go to Africa, she still would have been alive," he argued.

"Mr. Stone, your wife went there because she believed in a noble cause, but her death was a total accident. There's no one to blame," I said, trying to calm him down. "Just give me the gun, and we can help you out. Remember, your children still need their father."

I could feel that my words were getting into him. He lowered the gun a little, but then I watched as his eyes darkened again and his face reddened with anger.

He rose his gun again with a sudden move. "I lost my wife and my children because of this stupid auction. Someone has to pay for this. He has to die!"

He was about to pull the trigger, but I reacted faster than him. I fired a bullet that tore its way through his chest, causing a gaping hole from which blood started oozing profusely. He collapsed to the ground, his back facing the ceiling.

Taking a hard, deep breath, I eyed the lifeless body that was now surrounded by a pool of blood. There was no point in checking his pulse.

I lowered my gun and turned to Mr. Miller, who was pale and had very wide eyes.

"Mr. Miller, are you okay?" I asked.

He nodded without saying anything, as he was probably in shock.

Liam abruptly entered the room, followed by the rest of the team. He stopped in his tracks when he saw the body. He let out a breath before he turned to me. "Are you okay?"

"Yes," I gave him a quick answer before I hurried outside of the room as I felt it was getting harder to breathe...

***

I watched as some paramedics put the body bag in an ambulance to take it to the morgue.

Liam came into view and stood next to me. "I know it's hard."

I looked at him with a raised eyebrow, even though I knew exactly what he was referring to.

"Don't act like you don't know what I mean, Alex. The first time is always hard, but you can't let it get to you. Just remember that you had no other choice, and that you saved an innocent man today," he told me before walking away to speak with some other agents.

I always thought that I was prepared for a moment like that, but clearly, I was wrong.

I knew I had no other choice and if I hadn't pulled the trigger, he would have killed Miller and probably killed himself after.

I knew I did the right thing; however, taking someone's life and being the reason they stopped breathing was still hard, no matter what the reasons were. And the fact that it was justifiable didn't help in making it any easier.

Chapter 7

Watching as another agent left the office, I sighed.

The place was unusually calm as it was a Friday evening so most of the agents who still had lives outside of this building had already left.

I was finishing some paperwork and decided to stay overtime at the office. However, I had no open cases, so nothing was actually holding me back from leaving, but I wasn't entirely sure if it was a good idea.

I would love nothing more than to go home and get some pleasant sleep without having to wake up early for work. However, a constant reminder kept nagging me about not being able to sleep without having a dreadful nightmare, waking me up in the middle of the night. Something that made sleep feel more like a method of medieval torture.

I had no idea why I kept having those nightmares, and I felt they were pushing me to the brink of madness.

The number of sleeping hours I was getting was nearing zero, day after day.

I even had a feeling that I started seeing unreal things like that man with the tattoo at the auction—he must have been some kind of hallucination. There was no way he could be real.

My train of thought came to a stop when I heard someone clearing their throat near me.

Glancing up, I saw Ava looking at me with a raised eyebrow.

"What?"

"You look like hell," she stated, her eyebrows brought together.

I let out a sigh. I was very much aware of that little fact. There were large dark circles under my eyes from the lack of sleep, which I failed to hide with makeup. And my hair was frizzy and unkempt, even though it was in a messy bun. So yes, I looked like hell.

"What's wrong?" she asked. "Oh, and don't say it's work-related. I know this job can be hard, but I feel like there's something else going on with you, Alex."

I wanted to tell her. I wished I could share what I was feeling with someone, but I couldn't do that without telling them everything that had happened. And I wasn't sure if I could do that.

"Nothing," I lied. Then I changed the subject. "Do you have any plans for the night?"

"Yes, Caleb and I are going to a nearby bar to have a drink, and you're coming too," she said with finality, taking the file that was still in my hand. Then she tossed it inside one of my drawers. "Get off your ass now. And please do something with your hair."

I frowned at the last part, but I decided to go with them. Having a drink didn't sound like a terrible idea, and maybe a night out would help me ease up a little...

***

We went to a bar that wasn't far away from the FBI building. I figured out that most of the agents hung out there after work. Ava and Caleb had a group of friends already waiting for them. I sat and chatted with them for a while. But then the noise of so many people talking at the same time made me feel like my head was going to explode. So I excused myself from the table.

I wasn't really that much of an introvert, but this wasn't one of my best times.

I walked to the bar and ordered a shot of tequila. The bartender put the glass in front of me with a flirtatious smile. I gave him a sharp look that made him swallow hard and look the other way.

I swallowed all the tequila in one gulp. I put the now empty glass on the table before I asked for another shot.

I kept doing that until I lost count of how many shots I had, and now I thought I must be very intoxicated because everything seemed to be in a blur...

I stopped by the bar to grab a drink and play some darts for a while before heading home.

The first thing my eyes fell on when I walked into the bar was Alex, who was sitting alone and had her head in her hands. I walked toward her and sat on the chair that was beside her before I ordered a glass of bourbon.

She didn't even notice my presence, and I figured out why when I saw all the empty glasses that were in front of her.

"Are you trying to get yourself to pass out?" I spoke up, trying to grab her attention.

She removed her hands and looked at me, then she brought her eyebrows together in a frown. "What are you doing here?" she slurred.

"It's a miracle that you still recognize me." I looked at her with a slight smirk as I tried to lighten up the mood a little.

She said nothing in return and kept looking at something that I thought she only could see.

"I'm tired," she finally said. Her brown eyes looked darker than usual, and they no longer had the usual spark that always made them glow like a beautiful, starry night.

"Come on, I will drive you home," I said as I rose from my seat, grabbing her hand.

She didn't stand up or even move. "I'm tired of keeping everything inside all this time. I feel like there's something heavy weighing down on my chest, and it's getting very hard to breathe."

My eyes slightly widened. I had no idea what she was talking about, but I could feel the pain in her words. I sat back before I concentrated my attention on her. "Alex, what is it?"

She looked at me with eyes full of uncertainty. "I never wanted anybody to know, but I really need to talk to someone. I can't hold it in anymore. I feel like being trapped in a cage or as if someone's keeping me hostage."

"You can tell me." I reached out and put my hand on hers, trying to encourage her to speak as I wondered about the thing that was weighing her down.

"I have told you before that my father was also an FBI agent," she began, shifting her gaze away so she wouldn't be looking at me straight in the eye.

"Yeah, I remember that."

She took a deep breath before she continued. "I was ten when it happened. I woke up one night to the loud sound of gunshots. When I walked out of my room, I found four masked men surrounding something. When they moved, I saw the body of my mom—she was in my father's arms, and she was dead. Her blood was... everywhere."

I had wide eyes when she finished. I couldn't imagine what she had been through.

I watched as she breathed heavily and closed her eyes before she started to speak again.

"My dad saw me and looked me in the eye. I can never forget the look that was on his face. After that, one of them walked closer and pointed his gun at my dad's head. He muttered a few words to him I didn't hear, then he killed him with a bullet that went straight to the middle of his head." She turned to look at me. "I screamed and ran from them. I hid in the closet until the police found me."

"Alex, I'm so sorry," I whispered. She went through hell, and I couldn't grasp that she had kept all of that inside without having the weight of it crush her down.

"No." She shook her head slowly, looking me in the eye. "Don't give me any pitiful or sympathetic looks. I don't need them. I only told you because I want to sleep without having those nightmares again, to ease that pain a little so I can breathe."

I nodded silently, not knowing what to say. I watched as she grabbed the full glass that was still in front of her and gulped it down. Then she put her head on the table and closed her eyes.

I kept looking at her for a few moments, then I grabbed my own drink and thought about everything she had told me.

She was so strong. I couldn't believe that she managed to tell me all of that without breaking down. But I was really glad that she shared with me some of the things that were causing her a great deal of pain.

For I knew that the harder a person kept trying to keep something like that only for themselves, the bigger it would get. Until it would eventually take the form of their worst nightmares, an inner beast that would haunt and consume them whole.

Some battles were just never meant to be fought alone.

Chapter 8

A few sunrays pouring from the cracks of the blind fell on my face.

Trying to open my eyes, I winced and closed them back again quickly.

I knew people were sensitive to light when they woke up, but this was different. I felt as if someone were holding a torch right in front of my eyes.

Bringing my hands up, I pinched the bridge of my nose. I had an excruciating headache, as if someone were squeezing my skull tightly. And that wasn't everything. My mouth was parched, making me wonder if I had swallowed a dozen cotton balls by mistake. And I felt like I had received a hundred punches straight into my stomach.

My current condition was probably the literal description of death warmed over—only it wasn't so warm.

Blinking several times, I finally opened my eyes. I pushed myself to a sitting position with difficulty and looked around the room.

Something seemed off, but I couldn't put my finger on it.

It took me a while of more blankness and cluelessness until I finally figured it out...

This wasn't my freaking room!

Jumping out of bed quickly, I immediately regretted it when the room started spinning and I fell back onto the bed. I closed my eyes and held my head for a couple of seconds, trying to ease the dizziness.

I stood up again, slowly this time, so I wouldn't lose my balance again. Looking at myself, I found I was still in the same clothes I was wearing yesterday except for my blazer, which was on the bed, next to where I was sleeping.

What the hell happened?

The last thing I remembered was that I went to a bar with Ava and Caleb, then I had a shot of tequila, or maybe they were shots—lots of them.

I groaned. I felt gross, and I was dying to take a shower, but that was the least of my concerns right now because first, I had to figure out where the hell I was.

Walking out of the room slowly, I found myself in the middle of a modernly furnished apartment. My eyes wandered around for a while until they settled on the kitchen. What I saw there caused my eyes to widen, and my mouth almost hit the floor.

There stood Liam, shirtless and making breakfast. My eyes automatically wandered to his well-built body and defined abs.

I shook my head to regain concentration and returned to think about what the hell happened that led me to this situation.

"Oh, you're awake."

Liam's voice snapped me out of my thoughts.

"Y—Yeah," I muttered, looking at him sheepishly. I was trying so hard to remember what happened.

"I met you at the bar last night. You somehow got yourself stumbling drunk, and then you passed out," he explained, probably noticing the perplexed expression on my face.

"I don't know where you live, so I brought you here. And don't worry, I slept on the couch," he said with a slight grin.

A few pieces of yesterday's events hit me like a bus, making me wish for the ground to open up and swallow me down. I was still trying to prove myself to him and show him I was a good agent, yet I ended up being so wasted that he had to drag my ass home.

I slapped my forehead mentally. Why the hell would I do that? And what the hell did I do when I was intoxicated? Or say...

My eyes widened when I started remembering the conversation I had with Liam the other night.

"Hey, are you okay?" Liam asked.

I could really see genuine concern in his eyes. I locked eyes with him for a few seconds, saying nothing, still taken aback by what I had told him.

"Y—Yeah," I finally uttered, my tone a little low. Before I continued, I took a deep breath. "I'm really sorry, Liam. I have probably caused you a lot of trouble."

He gave me a soft smile. "You didn't cause any." Then I watched as his smile turned into his trademark smirk. "Besides, it was good seeing Miss Know It All a little drunk. Maybe I should have taken a picture."

I gave him a genuine smile, but it was shortly gone when my mind drifted back to what I had told him. "About what I told you yesterday, it's—"

He interrupted me before I could continue. "I will not open up that subject again unless you feel like talking, okay?"

I was a little taken aback by this side of him as I wasn't used to it, but a part of me felt like I could really trust him, and I found that to be strange. I had never felt that way toward anyone before.

"Thank you." I gave him a grateful smile.

He returned the smile, then he seemed as if he had remembered something. "I was just making breakfast. Would you like something to eat?"

I felt a nauseating feeling at the mention of food. I made a sad face before replying. "Well, I don't think my stomach finds breakfast an appealing idea at the moment."

He chuckled. "I will bring you an aspirin. It should ease the headache a little," he said. Then, he disappeared for a while and came back fully dressed, a couple of aspirins and a cup of water in his hands.

I took them from him with a grateful smile and gulped them down quickly, hoping they would help with the grumpy headache that felt more like torture.

He walked back to the kitchen. "Hey, what does your stomach think of the idea of coffee?" he asked, gesturing to the coffee pot in his hands.

"I think coffee doesn't sound so horrible?" I said, but it sounded more like a question, as I feared my stomach was going to disagree with me.

Liam chuckled a little as he poured us two cups of coffee.

My eyes wandered a little around the apartment as I waited for him to return with the coffee. They fell on a wall-mounted table that caught my attention. It had a couple of photographs and some other stuff on top of it.

I looked at the photos in intrigue. One of them was a picture of who I guessed was a little Liam with his family, and the other one was of Liam and another guy who seemed to be close to him.

"Here," said Liam as he handed me the cup of coffee.

He caught me staring at the photos. Great, now he must think that I was nosy above everything else. But I sighed in relief when I looked up at him and saw that he looked relaxed, and a slight smile was still playing on his lips.

"That's my family," he said, gesturing to one of the photos.

"You were a cute kid."

"I used to get into a lot of trouble."

"Why am I not surprised?" I gave out a little chuckle before I looked at the other photo. "Is this your brother?" I asked, pointing at the photo of him and the other guy.

I watched as his smile dropped and he stared at the photo for a while.

"No, he was my partner," he spoke up, not looking at me.

I was a little surprised. "I thought you didn't work with partners."

"I did. Once." He let out a little sigh, still not looking at me. "He was also my best friend. We got into the FBI academy together, and we became partners after graduation. The partnership didn't last for too long, though. He died in the line of duty."

My eyes widened. I was startled and didn't know what to say. "Liam... I—I'm sorry."

He gave me a slight smile, then he looked at the photo again. I knew his mind must have taken him on an unpleasant trip down memory lane.

"We were assigned to a case. A teenage girl was abducted, and we managed to figure out the identity of the kidnappers and their whereabouts. They were keeping her in an old, abandoned house.

"We made it there and were supposed to wait for backup because we didn't know exactly how bad the situation was. But then we heard loud screams coming from inside the house and we knew the hostage must have been in imminent danger. So we rushed to the house and raided it alone, without backup."

"Liam, you don't have to," I tried to tell him because I knew exactly how uncomfortable it would feel to talk about something like that. Also, he didn't have to share such a secret with me just because I shared mine with him.

"No, I want to," he told me.

I nodded in understanding.

He shifted his gaze away once more. "When we entered the place, we found ourselves face to face with a handful of armed men. We put up a really hard fight, but as they say, abundance overcomes courage. We both got shot. My shot wasn't fatal, but my partner wasn't as lucky as I was. He received a shot in the chest; the bullet pierced through his heart, causing him to breathe his last breath instantly at the scene." He looked at the ground. "The loss... I couldn't handle it. I blamed myself for a long time because nothing like that would have happened if we had just waited for backup."

Looking at him softly, I knew exactly how hard that could be. I took a step closer to him and put my hand on his. I felt he was a little surprised by my sudden touch.

"It wasn't your fault. I understand you couldn't stand still when you heard the hostage screaming. I probably would have done the same thing."

"I didn't want to be always reminded of what happened, so I asked to be transferred, and that's why I moved to New York," he said, then he looked at me with a half-smile. "Here you go; now you know why I moved to New York, and why I didn't want to work with partners."

Giving him a compassionate smile, I decided not to add anything else. He was right. Now, I had a better understanding of why he hated working with partners. He was too afraid that the past might repeat itself again.

Liam put on a façade that made most people think he was harsh, cold, and arrogant. But I believe that version of him was only a shell and a self-defense mechanism more than anything. He didn't want to get himself attached to anyone. And now, I really could see that he had a totally different side to him—a side that was perhaps his most genuine self.

I stayed for a while more with Liam. We decided not to broach those subjects again, so we talked about random stuff, and we finally started getting to know each other better. After that, Liam drove me home because my car was still parked in front of that bar.

The first thing I did when I made it home was to take a long, warm shower, then I put on a comfy pajama before I crawled under the covers.

Thoughts about Liam and what happened overwhelmed me as I lay down in my bed.

I knew I had some trust issues, and I never opened up to people easily. But, I really felt that I could trust Liam even though we haven't spent a long time together.

Yawning, I felt my eyes becoming heavier. I rolled over in my bed and closed them.

Eventually, the hustle and bustle of New York faded, and I was sleeping deeply.

I didn't remember having any nightmares that night.

Chapter 9

This's a bad idea. This's a really bad idea!

I thought as I stood in front of the main door of the house that witnessed the agonizing memory that haunted me everywhere.

I wasn't sure what exactly I was doing. I woke up today with a sentimental feeling and something inside told me I had to make this visit. The next thing I knew was that I was in my car driving to Brooklyn. And here I was, standing in front of my old home, not daring to take another step forward.

So many people advised me before that I had to visit the house. They told me that revisiting the scene of the trauma could help me get some kind of closure and move on, or even bring me some peace. I just couldn't...

However, I knew it had helped my grandmother. She cleaned the house after it was no longer considered a crime scene and used to spend long hours there whenever she felt like missing my father.

I remembered her going out for long hours and then coming home with red, puffy eyes. She said that she could feel his presence there. I was still young and thinking of that scared the hell out of me. I thought the house became haunted. Besides, I believed this might have worked with her because she didn't actually see them die in there.

Feeling overwhelmed with the memories, I was about to get back into my car, but something made me stop in my tracks. I looked at the house once again and made it closer to the door. I put the key into the keyhole with shaky hands before I turned it slowly. The door opened, and I felt my heart hammering inside my chest. I swallowed hard and took slow steps inside.

Finding the light switch, I turned it on. The first thing that my eyes fell on was the place where everything happened. My heart pounded even harder, and my breath felt like it was being ripped out of my lungs.

Although my grandmother made sure that everything was wiped, cleaned, and looked as if nothing had happened here. I could still clearly see the large pool of blood that surrounded the lifeless bodies of my parents, and their blood scattered everywhere.

A nauseating feeling crept through my abdomen when I felt the house was still scented with the smell of blood and death mixed with gunpowder.

I tried so hard to pull myself together and to hold it on, but I couldn't. I felt all my walls and masks coming tumbling down, as I couldn't hold the burning tears in my eyes any longer. A sob escaped my mouth, followed by a few teardrops, but they soon turned into a shower of salty tears that streamed down my cheeks, and my loud sobs echoed through the house.

Everything turned into a blur as I broke down completely. I felt that every tear was releasing some of the sadness, sorrow, and pain that had been trapped inside of me for too long, for I was always too terrified to confront them.

It felt like hours have passed, and I was still crying. I cried until I was no longer able to.

Currently, I was sitting on the floor, motionless. However, I was surprised at the sense of relief that had dared to creep into me.

Taking a deep breath, I started looking around me. And I realized I was no longer only seeing a scene of a trauma or a crime. I was seeing my old home; the one I grew up in and was a witness to a lot of my pleasant childhood memories.

Standing up, I started wandering around the house. Every part reminded me of a sweet memory. I remembered my mom standing in the kitchen, smiling at me while making my favorite cookies. And when my dad used to come home after a long, tiring workday. I would run to him, and he would carry and wrap me in a hug.

I walked upstairs and got into my old bedroom. I could see my mom reading me a bedtime story, then falling asleep next to me. Then, I went into my father's study room. It was his own little office; he used to spend a lot of time there looking through his cases. I smiled as I remembered all the times I begged him to tell me about his adventures at work and about the bad guys he caught and put away.

I felt so nostalgic. Those memories had a bitter-sweet taste, yet they brought a smile to my face.

I wandered around the office a little and decided to check my dad's desk. I opened the drawers and looked through them; they had many files and reports of cases.

One of them, in particular, caught my attention. The file had nothing inside of it except for a few pictures of victims murdered in different ways. Yet all the crime scenes had something in common—a mark that looked like a symbol. It was either carved on their bodies or painted with blood. I tried looking for anything else related to the case, but I couldn't find any. It looked like a case of serial murders, but the file didn't have any information or details except for those pictures.

Looking at my watch, I was surprised by how late it was. I couldn't believe I had spent the whole day here. I stood up and decided to take the file with me, as the case had piqued my interest.

I went downstairs and walked to the door. I gave the house one last look before I stepped out. With a loud bang, I closed the door behind me. It felt as if I were shutting the door of the past behind me.

Looking at the house one last time, I let out another sigh as I got into my car and started driving away.

After I went home, I started looking through the internet for information about the case. I felt disappointed because all I found were a few articles about the victims and the fear of a new serial killer wandering the streets of New York. I also found out that the mark was a Chinese symbol, meaning strength and power. This meant that the unsub was daring enough to leave a sign of power on his victims.

I did not know why I was so interested in that case, but I really wanted to know more, so I decided to look for more information about it at the bureau.

***

"Where did you get those?" Wyatt asked with a raised eyebrow while looking through the photos.

"I found them between my father's files." I shrugged, telling him the truth.

His eyes widened a little. "You went to the house?"

I nodded, saying nothing.

He sighed and looked at the photos in his hands for a while, then looked back at me.

"There were a lot of agents assigned to this case, including your father, who was really interested in it," he said. "At the beginning, we suspected it was the handiwork of a new serial killer in town, but it was just an assumption because we had no leads at all. We kept investigating and going through every little detail, but it was useless. The murderer didn't leave any piece of evidence behind."

"Did it turn into a cold case?" I asked, hoping for a negative answer. The number of cold, unsolved cases was really disappointing, especially those of a horrifying nature.

"Well, you can say that," he answered vaguely.

I raised an eyebrow in confusion.

"We figured out that we weren't dealing with a serial killer, but a whole crime network."

"The mob?" It made sense. Crime organizations tended to leave a sign of power on their victims, like cutting body parts off or leaving marks and signatures.

He nodded. "The case isn't ours anymore. Organized crime took charge of it, but they haven't made any progress nor found any useful information about the mob to this day."

I nodded in disappointment.

"Why are you so interested in that case, anyway?"

"I don't know. Maybe I was just curious to know more about it." I shrugged, then I stood up and gave him a polite smile. "Thank you for your time, sir."

I was about to walk out of the door, but Wyatt called for me.

"Alex, wait."

I turned to look at him.

"We went through every case your father worked on. We investigated and interrogated dozens of people, but we couldn't find anything that would lead us to the bastards who did it." He swallowed hard, looking at me with sorrowful eyes. "You should really move on, Alex. It has been a long time and I'm sure James and Olivia would have wanted you to move on, too."

I sighed. "I know," I said, giving him a forced smile. "Thank you again, sir."

I rushed out of the office before he could get the chance to add anything else.

Throughout my whole life, I always wondered how I could ever move on from the murder of my own parents, knowing that the people who did it got off scot-free.

And every time, I ended up reaching the same conclusion. All I could do was live with the memory, for I was afraid that moving on would never be an option for me...

Chapter 10

Growing up, my father taught me that there were no monsters lurking under the beds, sharpening their claws to rip their prey to pieces.

The real monsters walked among us every day and went unnoticed because they looked no different from us. They were humans who were capable of doing the most heinous acts imaginable.

However, after that day, I got too caught in the fires of grief and hatred. I believed that the monsters I once thought lived under my bed had crept from underneath it and leaped into my brain.

One of those monsters was my old home, where all the dreadful things had taken place. But when I finally dared to face that monster, I realized it was all in my head, because the real monsters were still out there, roaming the world, free and unscathed...

A few weeks have passed since I visited the house, and I had to admit that it kind of helped me. My feelings had become vivid, which allowed me to process and handle them better. The nightmares had diminished in intensity; that in itself said a lot.

And I had to keep myself from thinking about that bizarre symbol case after the conversation I had with Wyatt. I did not know why I was so interested in it in the first place, but maybe because I knew my dad showed interest in it, too.

Nevertheless, there weren't a lot of clues when it came to it, and I knew it couldn't have had anything to do with my parents' murder. There were no marks left on the bodies or even anywhere at the scene.

So in the end, I figured that dwelling on a cold case that had little to no leads was just going to be a waste of time, yet a part of me just couldn't help itself...

Running my fingers through my hair, I let out a bored huff. I was currently trying to finish some of the boundless paperwork related to cases Liam and I had solved.

I looked at the mountain of files in front of me in resentment and cursed under my breath.

I was desperate for a new case, and that made me feel a little bad. A new case would mean someone was dead or in danger, but I really needed to get out of the office one way or another.

Out of the corner of my eyes, I noticed an agent making his way toward my desk, a file in his hand. I allowed a fragment of hope to creep into me.

He finally stopped at my desk. "Agent Ryan, a man was found dead on a nearby street. NYPD insisted we should be involved. Will you and Agent Hunt look at it?"

"Sure," I spoke up, a little too excited than I intended to.

The agent looked at me with a raised eyebrow, obviously amazed by my sudden enthusiasm. "Okay, then you better get going because they are still analyzing the crime scene."

He handed me the file and walked away after giving me one last skeptical look.

He must have thought I was a freak for getting so excited over a murder case. I wouldn't try arguing with that, though.

Rising from my seat, I put my blazer on and started walking toward Liam's desk while reading through the file.

I made it to his desk and looked at him with a lopsided smile. "We have a new case."

He gave me an amused look, and I saw his mouth twitch into a little smile.

"I don't see the reason behind the smile, though."

I sighed. "I'm desperate for something that would keep my mind occupied. And I need an excuse to avoid all the paperwork for a while."

"Fine, what do we have here?" he asked, the smile still playing on his lips.

"A man was found dead on a side street a few hours ago, and the NYPD believes we should look into it."

He nodded and stood up from his seat, putting his suit jacket on.

"Oh, and I'm driving this time," I told him, waving my keys in front of his eyes.

He had a worried look on his face, but he knew better than to argue about it. So he just gave up, letting out a sigh, then walked next to me in silence toward the elevator.

***

We made it to the crime scene in a short time, as the crime had taken place on a nearby side street.

The scene was marked off with the familiar yellow police tape. And there were officers everywhere alongside the forensic team who were busy collecting evidence from the crime scene.

A lot of curious pedestrians were filling the area, trying to get a peek. We had quite a hard time passing through them before we could finally flash our badges in the face of a police officer who led us to the body.

My breath caught in my chest and my eyes widened in shock once they fell on the body.

The dead man was lying on his back, in a pool of his own blood that was now dry, gaining the color of a sickening shade of brown. He had a bullet wound in the area between his eyes and his t-shirt was torn off, revealing a mark that was carved on his chest with a hard object.

It was that same Chinese symbol...

Swallowing hard, I gazed at Liam. He looked as stunned as I was. I had already told him everything about that case, so he knew exactly what this meant.

Liam shared a quick look with me, then he cleared his throat and turned his gaze to one of the officers. "What do we know about him?"

"His name is Mark Lewis, 29. He had a long criminal record and was arrested many times for different charges. Drug possession, theft, assault," the officer answered.

"Who was the first to find the body?" I asked, kneeling down beside the body to have a closer look.

"Me," a man in a garbage collector's uniform answered. "I was collecting the garbage from those bins here this morning when I found the body."

Signs of shock were still visible on his man's face, so I simply nodded to that answer. Poor man, what a view to starting your day with.

I turned to one of the officers. "Did you find any bullet casings?"

The officer nodded, showing us a cartridge case wrapped in a plastic evidence bag.

I grabbed it from his hand and looked at it. Liam joined me.

"Ballistics confirmed the bullet came out of a .45 ACP," the officer said.

"We recognized this symbol the second we arrived at the scene."

Liam and I looked at the source of the voice. An officer who seemed to be older than the rest of his colleagues had just stepped into view.

He crossed his hands and directed his gaze toward the body. "It's not the first time I have seen it. So, I was sure the FBI would be interested, and that's why we immediately informed you."

Looking at him, I could tell from the look in his dark eyes that the long years he spent as a first responder had filled him with so much expertise and a lot of memories he probably wished he could erase.

I turned to look at the victim's body again, my eyes falling on the symbol over his chest. I sighed. The coincidence was mind-blowing.

"I don't believe in coincidences," Liam spoke as if he were reading what was going on in my mind. "This case fell into our hands for a reason. Maybe we're here now because we can find or do something the others couldn't."

"Yeah, maybe," I agreed, still looking at the symbol. Then I finally shifted my gaze and locked eyes with his blue ones. "I don't think being here would help us anymore. We need to look for leads somewhere else."

"I know. Maybe talking to the people who were close to him would help us."

I nodded in agreement.

We left the crime scene and kicked off with our journey to dig through the life that once belonged to our guy, Mark Lewis...

***

We found out that our guy lived alone, and the number of his family tree was close to zero. However, he had a close friend who was most likely the last person to have seen him alive. Lewis was seen hanging out with his friend in a nearby bar only a few hours before the predicted time of his death.

Liam and I wasted no time and went to that friend's house to talk to him. We knocked on the door a few times; a man in his early thirties opened the door. We showed him our badges.

"Sam Walsh. We're with the FBI and we need to ask you a few questions," Liam told him.

Walsh's eyes widened, and he quickly slammed the door in our faces.

Liam and I were a little taken aback by what had just happened, but we reacted quickly by pulling out our guns. The door was made of wood and not that strong, so Liam kicked it down easily. We walked in slowly, holding our guns tightly.

Sam Walsh was about to make an unthoughtful escape through the window, but he looked like he was stuck.

Liam and I both let out an exasperated sigh.

Liam walked to the window and pulled the man inside, then he cuffed him and read him the Miranda rights.

***

"So, Mr. Walsh. Do you know why you're here?" Liam asked, looking at the handcuffed man on the other side of the table coldly, his tone laced with authority.

The man shook his head, a smirk on his face. "I have no idea why the feds would be interested in me."

"Mr. Walsh, did you happen to know we found Mark Lewis dead early this morning?" I spoke up for the first time since we started the interrogation.

His eyes widened, and he looked like he had seen a ghost. He tried to hide his shock but failed. He swallowed hard before looking between us. "H—How did that happen?"

"He was shot in the head by a .45," I replied, maintaining my gaze on him. "We knew you were with him at some bar yesterday. We believe it was just a few hours before his death. Did he talk to you about anything? Maybe getting himself in trouble or receiving threats of any kind?"

"Nope," he answered, putting his cuffed hands on the table, making a clanging sound that echoed through the room. "All we did was drink beer and hit on pretty girls. Nothing more."

"Why am I not believing you?" I remarked, narrowing my eyes at him.

He smirked. "That's your problem, cupcake."

Feeling pissed off, I was about to snap at him, but Liam beat me to it.

"Listen, Sam," Liam said flatly. "We found a good amount of illegal drugs in your house, which is enough to make you spend a hell of a lot of time in prison."

The man looked paler as he swallowed hard.

"We are trying to solve a homicide case here, so if you help us by telling us whatever you know—and I'm certain you know something. We will consider offering you immunity or dropping the rest of the charges," Liam continued.

"Besides, don't you want to find whoever killed your friend?" I added.

The man looked at both of us with uncertain eyes. I could see that he was running our offer through his head. Torn between helping us and being labeled a snitch among his felon peers.

He finally scoffed. "Mark had done a lot of bad stuff that I can't even start to count, but he wasn't a murderer and he hated to get blood on his hands."

Liam and I shared a confused look.

"What do you mean?" Liam asked.

"Mark came to the bar yesterday and I could sense that something was off about him. He told me he saw two men killing another man before throwing his body into the river. He was terrified that they might have seen him." Walsh lowered his head and tried to hide the tremors in his hands as he moved them and folded them in his lap. "He was even willing to go to the cops and tell them about what he saw. But as you can see, they didn't give him a chance."

"Did he see their faces?" I asked.

"No, he told me it was too dark. But he heard them speaking a foreign language. He wasn't sure what it was, though," he replied.

I was about to ask something else, but the door of the interrogation room opened, and an agent walked in. He had light brown hair and green eyes, and he seemed to be around Liam. I didn't remember seeing him before, so he had to be from another unit.

"I'm sorry, Agents, but I'm afraid your time here is over," he said, looking between Liam and me.

"Excuse me?" Liam replied, raising one of his eyebrows.

"I'm Special Agent Ian Craven from the organized crime division," he said, showing us his badge. "This case belongs to us, so I'm going to take it from here."

Wyatt's words started hitting me. He told me that the organized crime division took over everything related to this case. That meant we were not allowed to work on it anymore.

Damn it!

Chapter 11

"**N**o. There's no way in hell I'm giving you permission for this!" Wyatt snapped, slamming a fist on the table.

He was obviously irritated for a reason God only knew.

"Sir, this case is ours. They can't just take the baton and leave us on the sidelines," Liam argued, gritting his teeth.

We both got so pissed off over what happened in the interrogation room and there was no way that we were going to give up on the case without a fight. We went to Wyatt and told him about what happened and asked him to allow us to work on the case, but unfortunately, he wasn't very fond of our idea.

"No, it's not yours. This case always belonged to organized crime," Wyatt said, giving Liam a hard look. Then his harsh, dark eyes darted at me. "Now that I mentioned it, I think I had previously made that clear to you, Agent Ryan."

I didn't give a reply, even though his statement succeeded in getting on my nerves. I took a peek at Liam, who was clenching his fist, and a flare of anger was clear on his face, gaining it a slight shade of red.

"And what the hell did they do with it all this time?" Liam demanded, a couple of veins popping out on his neck.

"That's none of your concern. It's their problem to worry about," Wyatt dismissed in a firm tone. Then he looked between the both of us with a stony stare. "Why do you really care about this particular case, anyway?"

I felt his words were directed at me. So, I finally stepped into the heated argument. I cleared my throat and looked at him.

"We're specialized in homicides, and it plays a huge part in this case. We could work alongside the organized crime division, and this isn't something new. A lot of divisions come together sometimes to solve different cases as part of a joint investigation," I said, hoping that I could convince him. "We could find something useful or make a difference, even if it was minor. This case has been open for so long, with no new leads. So why don't we just double our efforts? This may help us get hold of the tip of a new thread that might lead us somewhere."

"You said it yourself. This case has been open for so long that I don't believe you two can do anything better than all the agents in organized crime, and all the agents who worked on this case before," Wyatt said flatly, narrowing his eyes at me. "You should try solving some of the open cases that we have instead of wasting your time on a hopeless case." He looked between the two of us once again. "Our discussion is over. You can leave, now." He then made himself busy was some random file, a sign that meant he wasn't open to any further negotiation.

I looked at Liam, who was giving Wyatt a hate-filled look, and he seemed like he wanted to punch him in the face. I decided I wouldn't try to stop him if he planned to go on with it.

After we left Wyatt's office, a feeling of defeat washed over me. I was about to walk to my desk, but Liam stopped me.

He blocked my way. "Don't tell me you're going to give up."

"There's nothing we can do. Besides, he may be right. What's the difference that we can make?" It really had been a cold case for so many years, after all.

"Wow, I never thought you were the kind to surrender that easily." He scoffed.

A little smirk was playing on his lips as his blue eyes lit up with a mischievous look.

I narrowed my eyes at him, knowing that he was certainly planning for something.

"Let's go." He pulled my arm and started leading the way.

"Wait, where are we going?" I asked, having no option but to follow him.

"To the SAC's office," he said with a slight grin.

***

We stood in front of the closed door of Aaron McCoy's office, the Special Agent in charge of the FBI's New York office.

Liam knocked twice. We heard a voice calling for us to come in. He gave me an encouraging smile before walking in.

I took a deep breath before following him. I couldn't believe I had agreed to do this.

We stood in front of the huge desk in the middle of the office, feeling like misbehaving children.

The man behind the desk was looking at us skeptically. His dark eyes felt as if they were digging holes through us.

The wrinkles on his dark-toned face were like a map, telling the incredible journey of a man who had traveled through seven decades to this moment. A journey that was filled with long years of experience that certainly had gained him plenty of wisdom and prudence. I was in awe to be in his presence—the man was a veteran and a true legend to the bureau.

Liam cleared his throat. "Sir, I'm Agent Hunt and this's Agent Ryan. We're from the violent crimes unit, and we wanted to talk to you about something."

He looked at us with interest and gestured for us to continue. "Okay, go on."

We told him about everything, starting from being at the crime scene to what happened with Wyatt. He looked at us for a couple of moments, saying nothing.

I knew this was a bad idea. He would probably get both of us suspended for disobeying superior orders.

To my surprise, McCoy smiled. "Oh, I remember being as determined as you are when I was younger. Sometimes, I miss the excitement of the field."

Liam and I shared a hopeful look.

McCoy then focused his gaze on us. "But what makes you think you will be able to accomplish something all the agents who worked on this case before failed in?"

"Our specialty is homicides, sir. We can help the organized crime division by working on the murders," I said, hoping he was more willing to listen than Wyatt.

Crossing his hands, he leaned back in his chair and fixed his eyes on me, saying nothing. I could see that he was running everything we said in his head.

"Fine," he finally said after what seemed like ages.

Liam and I shared another look. We never thought it would be that easy or that he would even go for it.

"Sometimes change starts with a single person and that case has been open for so many years with no new leads. Fresh hands and eyes might be of help," he said with a faint smile.

We gave him a huge, grateful smile and thanked him before we excused ourselves.

He called after us. "Don't let me down, Agents."

"We won't, sir," I said with a determined tone before I closed the door of his office behind me.

***

We were on our way to our desks, feeling as if we were on cloud nine.

We were really grateful for what happened, and the chance McCoy gave us; however, that didn't last for too long, for we had to deal with a furious Wyatt.

He was standing upstairs and looked as if he wanted to strangle someone. "Hunt. Ryan. My office, now!" he yelled the second he spotted us, then he headed back to his office to wait for us there.

Words definitely spread around here really fast. Liam and I shared a perceptive look, both taking a deep breath, before making our way up the stairs to Wyatt's office.

"So, you went against my orders and went to the SAC!" he snapped, clenching his jaw.

"Sir, we just needed a chance," I argued.

"A chance to prove what?" He raised an eyebrow. "You both are good agents, but you're just going to waste your time. I can assure you, you will find nothing!"

I couldn't fathom why he hated the idea so much, but it was getting on my nerves.

"There's no shame in trying."

He gave me a stern look. "I hope you're not doing this because of another reason, Ryan. Because then you will be chasing after false hope."

His words stung, as I knew exactly what he meant. "Don't worry, sir. I don't have any hope to chase after," I uttered before excusing myself. I walked out of the office without even waiting for his permission. Liam followed me.

"Don't let what he said in there get to you," Liam said, walking beside me.

I nodded. "What do we do now?"

He smirked. "Now, we go and get ourselves a celebratory drink. I believe we have quite a long day ahead of us tomorrow."

I gave him a little smile. "That sounds good to me."

Chapter 12

Liam and I were on our way to the morgue.

We had been told that a body of a male was found floating on the water of the Hudson River. They thought he was the same victim Mark Lewis witnessed getting murdered by the hands of the same men who later killed Lewis, too.

We arrived at the morgue. Agent Craven was already waiting for us there. I could say that I was interested to see his reaction to having us work the case with him. Especially after the little argument that happened between us while interrogating Sam Walsh.

"Hello, Agents."

Ian Craven met us in the hallway, and to my surprise, he greeted us with a warm smile. I found it a bit odd because he was such a sour face when we first met him.

"I believe an apology is in order. I'm sorry about what happened when we first met in the interrogation room,"

Craven said. "This case is really challenging to deal with, and sometimes, it gets the best of you."

I gave him a little smile, deciding to put everything behind us. "We understand that. You don't need to worry about it."

He smiled back. "I believe we didn't have a proper introduction."

"Alex Ryan," I said, offering him my hand.

He shook it with a smile.

I noticed Liam was still giving him an intense look, so I decided to take care of the introduction part to ease the mood between them.

"And this is Agent Liam Hunt," I said, gesturing toward Liam.

They shook hands formally, both of them maintaining a hard look. Liam got so pissed off over what happened in the interrogation room. And that day, I found out that both of them were very good at verbal judo as they continued to argue for what seemed like forever. So, to be frank, I didn't really expect them to become best buddies.

"So, how did the autopsy go? Have they found any leads?" I asked, trying to break the bitter look they were both sharing.

Ian sighed and shook his head. "The body's in a terrible shape. I'll be surprised if we got anything useful out of it."

"I think we need to see it," Liam abruptly spoke up for the first time since we arrived.

"Okay, as you wish, but I can guarantee you, there isn't much to see." Ian shrugged, then he started leading us to one of the many rooms.

The body was lying on a metal table, the autopsy scars and marks were covering it. Inspecting it more closely, it seemed to me like there was a figure carved on his chest. But it wasn't easily recognizable as the water had dissolved it alongside most of the body's features.

I concentrated my eyes on it for a few minutes, running all the possible patterns in my head. I took out my note and sketched some of those patterns until I reached a very familiar one.

"Well, he's most definitely our guy," I said, capturing the attention of both Liam and Ian. I showed them what I found out.

"That damned symbol." Ian scoffed, clearly bothered by the fact that the list of the many victims of it just increased by one.

Although the symbol was in Chinese, the mob necessarily wasn't. We learned that over the years, organized crime had arrested, and was keeping tabs on a lot of people from different backgrounds and ethnicities, including many Americans. So the symbol only meant power and aimed to throw fear in the hearts and souls of whoever dared to stand in their way.

A man in a white coat walked into the room, grabbing our attention.

He approached us, a file in his hand. "Hello, Agents. I'm Doctor Jack Kent, a pathologist, and medical examiner," he started. "Our victim here suffered from many antemortem wounds and facial lacerations. That means that they beat him up pretty badly before killing him. He received a bullet to the skull, which was the cause of death."

"What about the carving on his chest?" I asked, focusing my gaze on the body.

The doctor looked at the report in his hand before he answered. "That was the only postmortem injury we found on the body."

So, the culprits took their sweet time with the body after making sure the man was dead.

Doctor Kent then held the victim's right hand and looked between the three of us. "As you can see, the fingertips are dissolved and most of the features aren't recognizable, so it was really hard to identify the body. But we ran an Odontology test and the matching results just came in. The body belongs to a man called Gerard Warner."

"Gerard Warner!" Ian repeated in a surprised tone.

"You know him?" Liam asked.

"Yeah, he owned a huge shipping and logistics company. We suspected him of being responsible for a lot of illegal trafficking using his company. We have been after him for a few years now, but unfortunately, we couldn't prove anything on him," he replied, disappointment clear on his face.

"It looks like you guys do an amazing job at the organized crime division," Liam said in a sarcastic tone, folding his arms.

Ian gave him a sharp look. Liam shrugged it off with a smirk.

I cleared my throat to get their attention and to save all of us the trouble of another argument. "Do you have any idea about the people who wanted him dead?" I asked, directing my question to Ian.

"Well, he definitely had many enemies. I will have to go back to the bureau and look through all the files we have on him," he answered. "But he was a married man. Maybe you can visit his wife and see if she knows anything that might be useful."

Liam and I agreed.

***

Liam and I were currently in the car, on our way to Gerard Warner's house.

"You don't really like Craven, do you?" I asked, a little smirk playing on my lips. Yet, of course, I knew I was questioning the obvious.

"I just think he's a little too full of himself," he replied, shrugging.

A laugh escaped my mouth.

"What?" Liam asked, raising an eyebrow at me.

"I just happen to know a thing or two about people full of themselves, and I don't really think you're in a place to judge." I grinned at him.

He narrowed his eyes at me, and that made me laugh even more. He just rolled his eyes at my reaction.

I went back to my serious mode. "Do you think we can really make any progress in this case?"

"I guess we will find out soon," he said, putting the car in park in front of an enormous mansion.

We walked toward the front door and rang the doorbell; a housekeeper opened the door. We showed her our badges and asked to speak with Mrs. Warner. She led us to a vast living room where we waited for her. After a while, a pristine-looking woman came into view. Although she was in her late fifties, she looked much younger and polished. I had an idea that a couple of plastic surgeries might have helped with that.

"Agents, how can I help you?" she asked, lips curling in what I thought was disdain.

Obviously, she was bothered by our presence.

"Ma'am, we need to talk to you about your husband," I started.

"Gerard... What about him?" she questioned, her posture becoming hunched. And I noticed the flicker of fear that clouded her eyes.

Liam and I shared a knowing look, as we figured out she had no idea about what happened to him.

"Mrs. Warner, can you please sit down first?" Liam asked her politely, taking by the rule of always asking people to sit down before delivering the bad news.

She looked between both of us in doubt before she took a seat on the couch in front of us, yet she was still restless.

"Mrs. Warner, I'm really sorry to inform you that we have found your husband's body this morning," Liam told her.

Her eyes widened, and she clasped her hand over her mouth, tears gathering in her eyes. "H—How did that happen?"

"He was murdered," I answered.

A sob escaped her mouth, and a few tears started rolling down her cheeks.

"Ma'am, I'm really sorry for your loss, and I know you need your time to grieve," I said, giving her a sympathetic look. "But we need to ask you a few questions that might help us in the case to find whoever did this."

She nodded, still breathing heavily. She grabbed a tissue and wiped some of the tears that had smeared her makeup.

She took a deep breath and looked at us with her red and puffy eyes. "He was supposed to be outside the country for things related to work. He told me he was coming home next week," she told us, her voice breaking. "I haven't heard from him for days, but I knew he always used to get distracted when he had his hands full of work. I didn't want to bother him, so I was just waiting for him to come back."

Things started to make more sense now. It explained why nobody looked for him or filed a missing report. Also, the fact that he lied to her about being abroad could prove that he had something to hide.

"Ma'am, your husband never left the country, and I'm afraid to tell you he might have been involved in some illegal business. That would actually explain why he had lied to you about his whereabouts," Liam told her.

Her eyes widened. "Gerard! T—That's impossible." She shook her head in disbelief.

"We're still running our investigations," I told her. "But do you know where he used to keep his important papers and files, or about the people whom he really trusted?"

She shook her head. "I don't know anything about any files, but I guess I might know the person who does. The person he trusted the most was his personal assistant; her name is Selene Williams."

"This might actually help us a lot. Thank you for your time, ma'am," I told her. "We will keep you updated if we figure out anything new."

"C—Can I see him? I—I mean the body," she asked, looking at us with eyes full of despair.

I shared a look with Liam before directing my gaze at her. "Of course, you could if you want, but... I don't really think it's a good idea," I told her. The body was hardly recognized. She could definitely spare herself that extra agony.

She nodded, probably understanding what I meant. We thanked her again, then we left the house.

After that, we went to the bureau and asked them to look into the assistant. We searched for her everywhere, but she was nowhere to be found, and she hadn't been home for two days.

We also searched her office in the company alongside Warner's office. We were lucky enough to find a few documents and stuff related to Warner's illegal activities in his personal safe. We also found out that Selene Williams was involved with him, and that made us able to incriminate her. Now, she was on the run, and a BOLO was put out for her.

***

Taking a sip of my cold coffee, I scrunched up my nose and put the cup away, letting out an exasperated sigh.

I was at the bureau, looking through all the documents we collected on Williams, trying to find something we might have missed before. But I still came out empty. We were desperate for any minor information that might lead us to her.

My landline telephone rang. I picked it up before the second ring. "Agent Ryan," I said through the phone. "What? Are you sure?" I asked with wide eyes. "Okay, thank you. We will be on our way." I rose from my seat and hurried to look for Liam.

I was just told that Selene Williams had been caught at LaGuardia Airport using an alias as she was trying to flee the country and leave for Canada. And now, she was in custody in one of the police departments that was near the airport.

Chapter 13

Liam, Ian, and I arrived at the police station where Selene Williams was being kept in custody.

She was trying to flee the country using an alias and a fake passport. But she didn't take into account the iris recognition system that was now used in most airports and could identify an individual only by scanning their eyes. She was arrested and sent to a police station that was close to the airport.

We introduced ourselves to an officer who led us to a middle-aged man. The latter smiled at us before introducing himself. "Welcome, Agents. I'm Lieutenant Jacob Morgan."

Liam was the first to reply. "I'm Agent Hunt, this's Agent Ryan and Agent Craven."

The lieutenant nodded, smiling at me and Ian. "The suspect is in our interrogation room. Let me take you to it," he said, gesturing for us to follow him.

We followed him to the observation room. I looked from behind the glass. Selene Williams was sitting on one of the metal chairs, looking distraught. She was picking at her nails, biting her lips, and looked haggard. Her blond hair was unkempt, and her blue eyes wandered all around her as if desperately trying to find a way out of the fate to come. And she looked young, probably around my age.

"Thank you, Lieutenant. We're going to interview her and take it from here," Ian said to the lieutenant, who nodded and left us in the room.

The three of us went into the interrogation room. She met my eyes evenly. I could tell that she was trying to flip an emotional mask on to hide her nervousness and appear calm. It didn't really work out well for her.

I sat in front of her without saying anything. Ian and Liam remained to stand, towering over me, and both made sure to radiate an intense vibe.

"Why am I here?" she asked, looking between the three of us. Her hands were shaking, and she looked on the verge of breaking down. I figured that a little push might do the trick.

"I suppose this's something you already know, Miss Williams," Liam answered her.

I knew he was fixing her with a hard stare without the need to look at him.

"Miss Williams, we know you were involved with Gerard Warner in his illegal activities. Acting clueless won't really do you any good," I added.

She gave us a bitter look but said nothing.

"You know that you're in an unpleasant situation, don't you?" Ian started. "You were involved with Warner. You can't deny that because we already have a lot of evidence to prove it. Also, you were caught trying to flee the country using a fake identity."

"Oh, and I actually find it a little uncanny that you disappeared right after your boss was murdered, which may suggest that you might have had a hand in it." I leaned back in my seat, giving her a pointed look. What I said wasn't true, but it wasn't frowned upon to lie in an interrogation if it was going to encourage a person to tell the truth.

And Voila, I got the reaction I was expecting.

Her eyes widened as she shook her head almost immediately. "What? No, this's bullshit. I would never hurt Gerard."

He was her boss, and she was calling him by his first name, which made me suspect that they might have had a thing going on between them.

"Were you romantically involved with him?"

My sudden question clearly took her by surprise. No words came out of her mouth as she opened and closed it a few times. She finally let down her guard and nod-ded. "It has been two years. His wife didn't know."

"Miss Williams, we're going to value your cooperation," Liam told her. "Just tell us what you know, and we will try to get you a good deal with the DA."

"Your time in prison can be reduced, and you could be sent to a minimum-security prison. You could find some comfort in there," Ian added.

She was looking between us with blue eyes full of uncertainty, as she was definitely running our offer in her head.

After a few long minutes, she clasped her hands in front of her on the metallic table before she started talking. "Gerard told his wife that he was going to be outside the country for a while, but it wasn't true. We were spending time together, and we were dealing with things related to... to our other business." She sighed. "One day, he went out to meet someone, but I don't know who exactly, and—and he didn't come back. I knew something had happened to him, but I wasn't sure." She paused to take a breath, and a few teardrops rolled down her cheeks.

"What happened next?" I asked, pushing her to contin-ue. I knew that the upcoming part was hard.

She swallowed hard. "I received a message—a threat. They told me that Gerard was gone, and I was going to meet the same fate if I ever decide to open my mouth," she said, and a sob escaped her mouth. She took a deep breath before she continued. "I didn't know what to do, so I ran. A friend of mine knows someone who can forge a passport. I—I didn't have any other choice."

I nodded. "Do you know any other things that can help us?"

She took a while to think, but she finally shook her head in disappointment.

"It's okay, but you knew a lot of things about Warner. Do you know anyone who might have wanted to hurt him, or even get rid of him?" Liam asked.

"I'm not really sure, but..." Her tone was laced with hesitation.

"Any minor information can be of help," Ian said, encouraging her.

"There was someone. Gerard used to do a lot of business with him, but I think they had a huge fight and a fall down as Gerard decided to cut off everything that linked them together," she told us.

"Do you know him?" I asked.

"I haven't really met him in person before, but I think his first name was Keith, Seth, or something like that. I can't really remember," she replied, a crease drawn on her forehead.

"It's okay, you have been a great help—"

A man in a grey suit abruptly entered the interrogation room, interrupting me.

"Excuse me, what are you doing questioning my client?" he hissed in an authoritative tone.

"Who the hell are you?" Liam snapped.

"Andrew West. I'm Miss Williams' lawyer," he answered, then he looked at Selene, who was giving him a look I couldn't decipher. He gave her a cup of coffee that was in his hand. "Here, I'm sure you need it after the interview you had with them."

I really hated lawyers!

He turned to look at us. "Can I speak to my client alone, please?"

I groaned. The three of us stood up and left the interrogation room before sending the lawyer a hate-filled look. Then we hurried to look for the lieutenant, as we weren't quite happy with him.

"Lieutenant, why didn't anybody tell us she asked for a lawyer? You know we can't interrogate her once she lawyers up," Liam hissed at the lieutenant.

"She didn't ask for a lawyer," the lieutenant replied. "I too found it odd when that lawyer came asking for her."

"Then how did he know she was in custody?" I asked.

"I'm not sure, but she used her one-time call. Whoever she called might have hired the goddamned lawyer."

The lieutenant sighed, looking at us with a guilty expression.

That explained it a little. Nevertheless, something still felt off about this, and I had an eerie feeling gnawing at my stomach. I even noticed that Williams was giving the lawyer a bizarre look.

"Unfortunately, we aren't even allowed to know what they're talking about." Ian shrugged before he took a seat.

I sighed before I found myself a chair too, as we all waited for the lawyer to finish whatever he was doing.

After a while of more dreadful waiting, the lawyer came out of the interrogation room.

"I'm done with her. You can go back to finishing whatever damage you were doing," he said, giving us a bitter smile. Then he stormed out of the office.

Yup, I really hated lawyers!

The three of us stood up and went back to the interrogation room. Once we were in the observation room, we saw Selene resting her head on the table motionlessly from behind the glass. We hurried into the interrogation room. Liam checked her pulse, but there wasn't any—she was already gone.

Pulling a napkin out of my pocket, I used it to hold the coffee cup and sniffed it. The infamous smell of bitter almonds was coming out of it.

She had been poisoned using hydrogen cyanide.

I noticed there was a paper folded beside the cup. I opened it and found out what I was already expecting.

That damned Chinese symbol.

Chapter 14

"**I**t didn't take three high qualified FBI agents to figure out that the lawyer was a fraud. He murdered her right under your noses. I can't believe it!" Aaron McCoy spat the words at us, anger and fury radiating from his eyes.

To say that we screwed up was definitely an understatement. We basically let that so-called lawyer kill Selene Williams while we were standing right in the next room.

"He showed the police a valid license from the state bar association. Besides, Williams didn't feel uncomfortable around him, and she said nothing when he showed up. We didn't have any reason to suspect him," Liam argued. "What should we have done? Checked the damn coffee ourselves!"

Liam's tone came out a little loud. I noticed a few veins popping out on his neck. He was starting to lose his temper and no good would come out of that. I silently prayed that he would keep himself in check.

"Agent Hunt!" McCoy called, dark eyes fixing Liam with a hard glare.

Liam apologized with a defeated sigh.

McCoy clasped both of his hands and put them on the table before he fixed his gaze on us. "I already know all of what you're saying, but you should have known better. You should have been extra vigilant, especially with this case," he reprimanded. "Any news about the lawyer?"

"We have screen footage of him and a sketch of his face everywhere, but there's no news about him yet," Ian answered in an apologetic tone.

McCoy nodded, then his eyes darted, giving me and Liam a stern look. "I really expected something good when I assigned both of you to this case. Don't make me believe I was wrong."

"We take full responsibility for what happened, sir. It was a huge mistake, and we definitely should have never let our guard down. But I can guarantee you, nothing like this will ever happen again," I said, silently praying that he wouldn't dismiss us from the case.

"I hope so," he said firmly. Then he gestured toward the door. "You can leave now, but notify me if anything new comes to the surface."

We nodded before leaving his office. The three of us went back to the floors of our divisions. Liam and I were told that Wyatt wanted to speak with us.

We both shared a knowing look before we headed to his office. I knew that our little failure must have made his day, and he probably wanted to gloat.

He gave us a mocking glare when we entered his office. "I heard about what happened."

I hated how smug he sounded, most likely believing that he was right about us not being a part of this case.

"We know that we could have done something about it, but it's a mistake that's definitely not going to happen again," I retorted.

I received another glare from him. Then he sighed, leaning back in his chair. "You still don't believe that you are wasting your time on that case?"

"No, we don't," Liam said, still sounding a little tense. "We have found lots of new threads, and we will not stop till we know where they lead."

Wyatt let out a sarcastic chuckle, which made my urge to punch him increase rapidly.

He pointed toward the door. "Okay, you can leave. I just wanted to know if you had grown some common sense after what happened. Clearly, you didn't."

Liam tightened his grip, and I understood. I really wanted to do the same. I grabbed Liam's hand before excusing both of us.

"You should have let me punch him," Liam told me once we were out of the office.

"Getting fired won't do us any good, will it?" I looked at him with a raised eyebrow.

Then I sighed and ran my fingers through my hair. "I'm really exhausted. This case is driving me crazy, and I'm afraid that we might have lost all leads and reached a dead-end all over again."

"Don't be pessimistic. We just need to clear our heads, and I happen to know a place that will help with that a little."

I gave him a skeptical look.

He chuckled. "You will like it, I promise."

I narrowed my eyes at him. "What exactly am I going to like?"

"You will know when we get there." He smirked before he turned on his heel and started making his way toward the elevator.

Letting out a sigh, I figured out that I had no option but to follow him.

We got into the elevator. It stopped at one of the floors. Ian got in. He looked a little surprised at finding the two of us in there.

"I was just coming to find you." Ian's words were directed at me. "Alex, you looked a little tired, so I thought we could grab a cup of coffee together and talk about the case."

I noticed Liam stiffening beside me, and I suddenly became uncomfortable.

I looked at Ian with an apologetic look. "That would have been great, but I already have somewhere to be. I'm sorry, Ian. Maybe we can do it another time?"

Out of the corner of my eyes, I could see Liam smirking.

Ian looked at me with a smile that I believed was bitter. "It's okay. Yes, we could do it any other time."

The elevator stopped. I gave Ian another apologetic smile. "See you later."

I stepped out of the elevator with Liam, and we walked together toward his car.

***

It took us twenty minutes to reach the destination Liam refused to tell me about. I was certain he enjoyed seeing me suffer from the curiosity that was eating me whole.

Liam parked the car in front of an old building. I got out of the car and looked at the building in confusion, wondering what could be interesting in there.

"Come on," Liam said, walking ahead of me toward the building.

"Not until you tell me what's inside." I froze in my place, crossing my hands. My curiosity was really getting the best of me.

"You will know, soon enough." Liam chuckled. "Jeez, have some patience."

Yeah, he was definitely enjoying this.

He walked inside without looking back. I groaned as I followed him.

I was surprised to see myself standing inside what looked like a huge training center. It was full of different equipment.

A muscled man with dark skin appeared from behind some large piece of equipment. He approached us, a wide grin on his face. "How are you doing, man? It has been a while," he greeted Liam.

"Yeah, I have been really busy for quite some time," Liam said as he pumped his fist with him.

Then Liam looked at me, a smile on his face. "Alex, meet Tom. He owns the best training center in the city." He waved his hands, gesturing to the training center we were currently standing in. "Tom, meet Alex Ryan. She's my partner."

"Hey there," Tom greeted me with a grin as he shook my hand. He then gave Liam a mischievous look. "But I thought you didn't work with partners."

An involuntary smirk took over my lips.

I looked at Liam, who grinned when he caught my eye.

"Well, people can change." He shrugged.

"Well, enjoy your time here, folks. You can have the whole place for yourselves," Tom said, then he looked at me. "For your information, Alex. You're the first girl Liam ever brings here." He winked at me before he left us and walked toward the door.

I noticed Liam giving him a sharp look that accompanied him until he was no longer in sight.

"Well, I didn't really expect that," I spoke up as I started walking around to take a better look at all the equipment.

A smile was flickering around the edges of Liam's mouth. "I can always manage to surprise you."

He walked towards a boxing bag and called for me to join him. "Come on, get it all out," he told me.

I raised an eyebrow at him. "Get what out?"

"I always come here to train when the job problems get too overwhelming," he explained. "You said you were exhausted. Get everything that is weighing you down out."

I looked at him like he was insane, but he ignored me and held the boxing bag for me, anyway. I scoffed before deciding to give it a try.

I punched the bag lightly, then a little harder, then much harder.

I felt that everything going on in my mind was getting out with every punch. So I punched the bag repeatedly while Liam was holding it until I could no longer breathe.

When I was finished, I was sweating and panting.

Liam came closer. "Our job is tough, and you can't let it get to you. If you do, it will take away pieces of you with it until you'll no longer be able to recognize yourself."

"It's not just about the job, Liam," I said through heavy breaths. "I feel like my mind is going to explode because of everything that's going through it. The case... I have a feeling that it may be linked to my father. I know it's a bit of a stretch, but I can't stop myself from thinking about it."

"Do you think it has something to do with what happened to your parents?"

"I don't know, I—" I sighed, running my fingers through my hair. "There's nothing linking the case to their murder but..." I paused, not finding the right words to say.

"Alex, you can talk to me about anything." He gave me a warm look that meant he was ready to listen to whatever was occupying my mind.

"I have this little feeling inside of me that I can't get rid of, no matter how hard I tried. A gut feeling telling me this case is linked to what happened to my parents somehow. Although, I can't help but feel that my mind is just playing tricks on me, trying to give me false hope." I sighed and looked away to avoid his gaze.

"You know, growing up, I had only one wish, and it was to find the bastards who did it and make them pay." Slowly, I looked at him and finally met his blue eyes, trying to find in them the reassurance I needed.

Liam kept looking at me in silence. He always knew when I wasn't in need to hear anything but to get what was inside of me out, to be listened to.

"Have you ever felt trapped? Like being in a cage that you created yourself, yet you still didn't have the key out. Throughout all my life, that memory never left me—ever. It was like my whole life stopped on that day and is now just revolving around it."

"After the incident that happened with Charlie—my partner. I figured out that no matter how much time I spent thinking about what had happened. For days, months, or even years, trying to collect the pieces, think-ing about what I could have done differently. It just wouldn't change anything," he said, looking at me with soft, compassionate eyes. "Letting go and moving on doesn't mean that you stop caring about the people involved. It's realizing that the burden of holding on is just too heavy, and the harder you try to grip, the greater the damage will be."

I kept looking at him, thinking about everything that he said. I couldn't even count the times I had been told to let go and move on, and I was never able to. But to my surprise, I found comfort in Liam's words. Or was that comfort in Liam himself...

He closed the gap between us, locking eyes with me. "Alex, I'm pretty sure your parents would've wanted you to be happy, and I know for sure they're really proud of you."

I felt a mix of emotions that I had never experienced before, and I couldn't even describe them. But the only thing I was certain of, at the moment, was that I was really grateful that my path had crossed with Liam's, that I opened up to him, and that he was currently here with me.

I didn't notice how close he was to me until the smell of his heady, woody cologne reached my nostrils. My heart pounded like a drum in my chest, and I could hear it loud in my ears.

I took a step back automatically. I expected him to move, but he didn't. He took a step closer and closed the gap between us once again.

He was looking straight into my eyes, his ocean blue eyes piercing through me. I stared back at him without moving a muscle.

Unexpectedly, his hands drifted to my hips as he pulled me closer. I inhaled sharply as I was right against his warm chest.

I wanted to push him away, but I couldn't. Or was it because I didn't want to?

His face came closer to mine and just when his lips were about to touch mine, his mobile rang, bringing both of us back into reality.

We both moved away quickly.

Liam nervously got out his phone before putting it to his ear. I didn't hear what he was saying, though. I had wide eyes and my heart felt as if it were about to jump out of my chest.

What the hell was about to happen?

Liam finished talking on the phone and turned to face me. "They say they have important news related to the case."

All I could manage was to give him a slight nod.

We left the training center in a hurry and got into the car, and he started driving back toward the bureau, both of us not daring to utter a word.

Chapter 15

Liam and I made it to the bureau after twenty minutes of a torturing car ride. It was filled with silence and tension that could be cut with a knife.

I had a hard time believing what was about to happen. It came out of nowhere and I had no idea that Liam thought of me in any way other than just being partners and friends.

I had to admit that we became quite close over the course of the last period, and we were now really good friends. He was one of the few people in my life I trusted and could be myself around. Not only that, but I felt he could always bring out the best in me, and even bring delight to my life. I was glad to have him by my side.

Still, what baffled me the most was that I didn't stop him and that my body felt as if it were screaming for that kiss. Was I developing feelings toward him? I mean, any girl would. He was ridiculously handsome. And although he made people think he was arrogant and cold-hearted all the time, it wasn't true. He was actually kind and sincere. But we were work partners and I couldn't be falling for him, could I?

Thinking about my past, I never believed that I ever had a genuine relationship before, or that I had experienced what falling in love felt like. But what I was currently feeling was so strange and overwhelming that I couldn't really put it into words.

I shook my head, trying to clear my mind, as I needed it to be well-functioning for the sake of the case.

We arrived at Agent Craven's office. He was going through a file, but he put it down the second he noticed us. "Hey, it's good you were able to return quickly."

"What happened?" Liam asked.

I could tell that he was irritated. And I noticed that he avoided looking at me through the entire ride here. I couldn't really blame him because I was basically doing the same thing.

"We have interviewed most of Gerard Warner's employees, and there's one thing they all agreed on," Ian began. "Apparently, Warner had a huge fight with one of his business partners a few days prior to his death. They say it was so heated that Warner had to kick him out, and he told the security to never let him step a foot in the company ever again."

"Did you figure out who that partner is?" I asked.

Ian smirked a little before he handed each of us a file. It had information about a man named Seth Mancini.

"Seth Mancini. He's of Italian descent. He owns a large group of casinos and hotels all around the country. What's so special about this man is that he's a renowned crime lord. He has been involved in drugs and arms trafficking, money laundering, counterfeiting, assault, and the list goes on." Ian shrugged as he summarized the file to us.

"And why exactly is that man out of prison?" Liam scoffed, raising one of his eyebrows.

"Things aren't easy with organized crime, as you may think. It's hard and sometimes even impossible to get rid of the bosses—the crime lords. They always find a way out. Like someone else taking the blame for them or making evidence disappear. They also have important acquaintances everywhere, even here," Ian said flatly. "And if you were lucky enough to put them in prison, that's not a problem, as they can make it their little empire. Even if they die, someone else always takes over. It's a cycle that never ends."

Liam narrowed his eyes to a squint but said nothing. He just concentrated his gaze on the file in his hand. It was good to see him speechless, though.

I looked at the file again and Mancini's picture caught my eye. It gave me an eerie feeling. He felt oddly familiar.

"I think we should pay him a visit," Liam finally said with a sigh, and we agreed.

***

We knew Mancini was currently at one of his casinos in the heart of the city. We headed there to ask him a few questions, and to see if he knew anything about what had happened to Warner. Although we knew it would be difficult to get the truth out of him, it was still worth a shot.

There were a couple of bodyguards standing in front of the casino. They were double the size of both Ian and Liam, and they were certainly armed. We flashed our badges in their faces and asked to meet Mancini. They gave us heated glares and went to inform Mancini about our presence. One of them came after a good ten minutes and motioned for us to get inside.

Loud voices filled my ear immediately, and the place was scented with the smell of alcohol and tobacco. Very few people noticed us as we passed by them as the majority looked intoxicated and the rest were busy gambling.

We followed the guard to a separate room. He opened the door and gestured for us to get in. It was an office, and Mancini was sitting behind a large mahogany desk.

He was in his mid-fifties. He wore a three-piece tailored suit that gave him the impression of the powerful businessman he aimed for. His hair was a mixture of salt and pepper, and he had a perfectly styled goatee beard. His eyes looked like those of a dangerous hawk, studying its prey. He was looking at us coldly as his lips twitched into a malicious smirk.

"I wonder what brings the feds to me this time," he said, clasping both of his hands. "How can I help you, Agents?"

"We need to ask you a few questions about Gerard Warner," Liam was the first to respond.

"Oh, poor Gerard. I heard about the unthinkable tragedy that happened to him. This's really sad. He was such a good man," he said in an obvious, fake, sad tone before he opened a box that was on his desk. He brought out a cigar and lit it.

I could see some kind of black ink on his right hand, but it was a little vague. I focused on it for a few seconds. My eyes widened in recognition, and I felt my blood turning to ice water in my veins.

It was that same tattoo...

Could it ever be possible?

I felt my heart racing inside my chest, and the oxygen was becoming scarce in the room with every second passing. I looked at Mancini again and I could see that he was looking at me, too. His cold, glassy eyes were making me feel bare.

I could see Liam looking at me with concern clouding his eyes.

He approached me and whispered. "Alex, are you okay?"

I wanted to say something, but no words came out of my mouth. I just nodded and hoped that he would buy it. He clearly didn't, as he kept looking at me with narrowed eyes.

"So, Mr. Mancini, how exactly did you know Gerard Warner?" Ian asked, drawing attention to him instead. I was thankful for that.

"He was one of my whales. He used to spend hundreds of thousands in one game," Mancini said as he put the cigar between his lips, then he blew the smoke carefully.

The smell made me feel nauseous.

"We heard about your little fight. Could you enlighten us about what happened?" Liam asked in a challenging tone.

Mancini gave us a sardonic look. He had to know that we were pointing fingers at him.

"It was nothing. I'm sure I would have seen him in the casino in no time as if nothing had happened. Well, if he hadn't gotten himself killed, of course." He drummed his fingers on the table, an enigmatic smile on his face.

"I'm sorry to inform you that you're looking in the wrong place. As I said, Warner was a high roller—his death cost me a lot."

"But he kicked you out of his office. Didn't you find that humiliating?" I found myself asking. It was the first time I spoke since we came here. "And what do you mean exactly by saying "gotten himself killed"?"

His smile turned into a frown as he looked at me, and I could see that I had gotten under his skin. He slammed his hands on his desk, looking at us sharply.

"If you have anything on me, you could arrest me right now. If not, then you're just wasting my time, and it would be great if you spared me the trouble and decided to leave," he seethed. "And the next time you come here, please remember to bring a warrant."

We left his office after giving him one last look that meant things were far from being over. We knew he was hiding something, and we had to figure it out no matter what.

We got into the car and Ian started driving back to the bureau. Liam concentrated his gaze on me every once in a while, but I didn't even bother to return the look. I was lost in thought.

I remembered that Mancini was the same man I had seen before in the fundraising auction with that same tattoo. Could it be a mere coincidence, or did I just face the man who brutally murdered my parents?

Could my hunch have been real all this time? Could this case have something to do with my parents' murder? Was I actually close to the people who did it?

At that moment, my head felt as if it were going to run into a short-circuit. Countless questions with no valid answers kept nibbling at it like a hungry rat.

All I knew was that there was something invisible, yet so strong tying me to this case. And I was determined more than ever. I had to find all the pieces of the puzzle and get to the bottom of the mystery, no matter what it took...

Chapter 16

I lost count of how many hours I have been sitting at my desk, going through endless files and documents about Seth Mancini. And that was only for today.

For the past few days, every agent working on the case had only one mission. Finding anything that would tie Mancini to Warner's murder. But we always came out empty, no matter how hard we tried.

His past was like an unsolved puzzle. He was suspected of every kind of crime someone could think of; however, he was only convicted of a white-collar crime once. And his attorney surely did a hell of a job as he served only two years in prison. Plus, it seemed like he started making a name for himself over the past ten years, as there wasn't much accessible information about him prior to that.

Mancini undoubtedly had the key to a lot of unsolved questions, but we had nothing on him. And if we ended up losing him, we would be back to square one.

Also, I still couldn't find anything that could prove Mancini's involvement in my parents' murder except for that tattoo. If I told anybody about that, they would instantly say that I was just blowing things out of proportion.

I sighed, stretching my body. The case was literally making me pull my hair out, and I seriously believed that there was a very thin line between me and a mental meltdown.

Rubbing my eyes with the heel of my hand, I held back a yawn. I grabbed the cup of coffee that was on my desk and took a sip. I grimaced at the cold taste. After dumping the rest of it in the trash bin, I decided to make myself a fresh, warm cup of coffee. I hoped an extra dose of caffeine would help me get through the rest of the day.

I walked to the coffee machine, and because I was tremendously lucky, I found out that it was broken. I hit the stupid machine and groaned loudly.

"Looks like someone is having a bad day."

I looked up to see Liam, a smile flickering around the edges of his mouth. I threw a look at him that made him shrug innocently, his smile never wavering.

"I would kill for a decent cup of coffee, too. What do you think about having a coffee break?" he suggested.

"Yeah, that would actually be great," I decided, even though I was feeling some hesitation inside me.

We have spoken little in the past few days, and it wasn't because I was trying to avoid him or anything. But we were both pretty busy with everything related to the case, and of course, we didn't have the chance to talk about that night in the training center. It was better this way, though; my mind couldn't take any extra pressure.

Anyway, we went to our usual coffee shop. We ordered two cups of double espresso, and then we chose a table that was in a faraway corner to drink our coffees in peace.

"So, what's really going on with you?" Liam asked abruptly, his blue eyes fixed on me—probably looking for any reaction.

"What do you mean?" I asked with a raised eyebrow.

"I knew something was bothering you since the day we interviewed Mancini, and don't say it's just the case. When we were there, you looked like you had seen a ghost," he pressed. "Do you know him personally?"

I looked at him for a solid minute, not knowing what to say or if I should tell him the truth. Finally, I sighed. "The tattoo that was on his hand," I started. "It was the same tattoo that the man who killed my parents had on the exact same spot."

Liam didn't look surprised. We had already talked about my suspicions about this case on that day in the training center.

"Do you think it's just a coincidence, or that he had something to do with the murder?"

"I honestly don't know what to think anymore," I answered truthfully, letting out a defeated sigh.

He nodded, probably understanding the fact that my mind at the moment was more like Times Square on a really busy day.

"Alex, I remember you telling me that your father worked on this case before and that he was pretty interested in it." He leaned on the table. "So, if we considered this, there actually might be a possibility that everything might be connected, after all."

"Yeah, but he worked on it only for a short time before it was reassigned to organized crime," I said. "Also, if it was related, it would have been likely to find that Chinese symbol anywhere at the scene or on the bodies, but there was no sign of it."

Liam nodded but added nothing. He, too, seemed to be in deep thought. That was the most puzzling part, and I couldn't find a satisfying explanation for it.

We drank our coffees in silence for a few minutes before Liam finally put an end to it once again.

"Alex, I know it might not be the right time to talk about this, but..." He paused.

I noticed that Liam was finding his coffee cup really interesting, as he didn't take his eyes off it. He seemed like he was struggling with words. However, I knew exactly what he wanted to talk about.

My heart rate increased as I recalled what happened that night in the training center in my head. Honestly, I had no idea what he was going to say, or even if I was ready to talk about it with him just yet.

I found myself looking at my wristwatch before I quickly spoke up. "It's getting late. We should probably get going. We need to get back to work." I immediately rose from my seat and tossed my now empty cup in the trash bin.

I glanced at Liam, who had a disappointed look on his face. He let out a sigh before he stood up and joined me without saying a word.

We were just getting out of the coffee shop when we heard the sound of a gunshot. We didn't have enough time to respond as a bullet missed me by a few centimeters and hit the glass behind me, shattering it to pieces.

Liam and I reacted quickly by pulling out our guns, then we hurried and hid behind one of the parked cars, taking it as a shelter.

I thought that my heartbeats had reached the speed limit as I was aghast by what just happened. But I knew it was definitely not the right time to freeze up, and I had to focus on our trigger-happy fellows. I glanced at Liam, who looked much calmer than me.

Multiple shots cracked through the air again, and the screams of panicking pedestrians filled the area. And at that moment, I felt that all my senses were sharpened by adrenaline. Things were getting hectic, and we had to do something before anybody got hurt.

Liam raised his head cautiously to get a view, then he lowered it back quickly.

"There are two of them, and they have machine guns," he told me. "I will try to distract them while you try getting a clear shot."

I nodded. Liam sent me a knowing look before he left his place beside me and went directly into the chaos.

I could hear the distinct sounds of gunshots. I prayed to God that Liam would be okay, that everyone would be okay, and that we could tackle the situation with no casualties.

Slowly rising to my feet, I now had a clear view of the situation. People were hiding inside the nearby buildings and behind cars, and children were crying while holding on to their mothers tightly. I felt a sense of slight relief when I heard the sound of sirens and saw the familiar blue and red lights of many police cars approaching the scene from afar.

I shifted my gaze to the shooters, who weren't concentrating on the place where I was hiding anymore, but on the place where Liam was shooting from.

I fixated my gun on one of the shooters. But before I could pull the trigger, an old man suddenly blocked my view. I saw him running toward the shooter I was aiming at as fast as he could with a stick in one hand. My eyes widened as I realized what he was doing.

"No, stop!" I yelled, but he didn't hear me. I quickly got out of my hiding place and hurried toward them, trying to get a good shot and not hurt the man in the way.

I wasn't quick enough.

On a spur of the moment, the shooter turned to face the man, aiming his gun at him. He fired two bullets, causing the old man to stagger before he fell to the ground.

I stopped in my tracks, but I didn't have any time to process what happened as the shooter noticed me and fixed the gun in my direction.

My reaction was faster than his. I immediately raised my gun and fired a bullet in his direction. I watched as he dropped the gun that was in his hand and collapsed to the ground.

The other shooter, who was on the other side of the road, panicked and backed away quickly. Liam chased after him. He got into a black SUV, and I heard the screeching of tires. Liam fired a few bullets toward the car, an act that was futile as he was already out of reach.

Hurrying toward the civilian who had been shot down, I kneeled beside him to check his pulse. There was none. I cursed and closed his eyes, which were wide open with a horrific look clouding them. I felt an ache in my heart—he didn't deserve to die.

Getting myself back up on my feet, I walked straight toward the bastard who I had shot. I found out that he was still alive and fighting for breath. I quickly took off my blazer and put it on the bullet wound, trying to stop the bleeding.

The police were already filling the area. "I need a medic, right here!" I shouted. A police officer immediately started speaking into his walkie-talkie.

I looked at the man again, who looked like he was about to get into shock. "No, I'm not letting you die today. You have got so many damn questions to answer."

Two medics quickly came into view and immediately loaded him on a gurney, and into an ambulance.

When the ambulance was gone from view, I finally let out a breath that felt as if I were holding it in since the whole thing began. And finally, I started to comprehend everything that had happened.

My eyes started wandering around the area. It was now filled with policemen and medics everywhere as they tried to help and find out if anybody was injured during the hassle. While the poor civilians were definitely petrified beyond words, not believing they had just gone through a mass shooting on what started for them as an ordinary day.

"Alex, you okay?"

Liam's voice shifted my attention toward him. He was now standing next to me, his eyes filled with concern.

I nodded. Yes, I was okay, physically; however, mentally, I was a mess. I knew he understood because he definitely had the same mix of emotions and thoughts haunting his mind.

After helping the police at the scene, we went directly to the hospital where the shooter had been taken. We were going to wait for him to recover so we can interrogate him and get all of our desired answers out of him.

This time, I allowed myself to have a tiny thread of hope. We were finally one step ahead of them...

Chapter 17

Groaning, I threw another now fully red napkin in the trash bin.

I was trying to scrub off the blood that I was covered in from my attempt to rescue the hatchet man, but it was to no avail. I decided to give up on the cleaning process for it had proved to be only a waste of time.

Letting out another sigh, I glimpsed at myself in the mirror. I looked like hell, but that was totally justifiable as it was only a few hours after being so close to getting assassinated.

I splashed some water on my face and pulled my dark-brown hair up in a bun before I walked out of the bathroom.

The scent of antiseptic and bleach filled my nostrils as I walked through the long corridor of the hospital. I noticed that people were staring at me with a suspicious look, but I couldn't really blame them. My clothes were soaked in blood, and I had a gun strapped to my waist. I didn't really have the FBI agent impression around me right now. Instead, I looked like a psychopath who was about to commit mass murder.

I finally arrived at the waiting room where Liam was waiting. He was on his phone, pacing back and forth as he talked with the person on the other end of the line. I sat on one of the chairs and waited for him to finish.

I noticed a doctor walking into the room. I recognized the look on his face. It was a look even we often used when we informed someone about the loss of their loved ones. I watched as he approached an elderly couple who were holding hands. He started talking to them. It didn't take much time before the woman clasped her hands over her mouth and started crying as her husband embraced her in a hug.

I wondered who they had lost.

"That was Craven," Liam spoke up, grabbing my attention to him. "He ran the shooter's DNA and found him in the system. He has all the information we need, and he's on his way here as we speak."

"Good," I said with a slight nod.

"Hey, you can go home, take a shower, and change your clothes if you want," Liam suggested. "There are enough police officers here to make sure that prick stays where he's supposed to be."

"No, I will wait." I shook my head, then I regarded him thoughtfully. "Who do you think might be behind what happened?"

For one, I knew it was definitely linked to the case, and it gave me a feeling that we were getting close to something important. Something they were so scared it might see the light of day that they had attempted to kill two federal agents over it.

"I don't know." He sighed, sinking into the chair beside me. "But I guess we will figure out soon enough. We're ahead of them, this time."

I nodded, saying nothing. I kept staring at nothing in particular. While Liam leaned back in his chair and rested the back of his head against the wall. The day had completely burnt us out.

Silence engulfed the room until another doctor entered the room and approached us.

"The patient is now out of surgery. The bullet hadn't damaged any vital organs; we were able to remove it without any severe complications," he informed us.

"When can we question him?" Liam asked.

"He's still under anesthesia. You can talk to him after he wakes up," the doctor answered.

We thanked him before he left. Then from afar, we noticed Ian walking toward us, and to my surprise, he had Wyatt with him.

"What's he doing here?" Liam asked, referring to Wyatt.

"I don't know, but it can't be good." I shrugged. Wyatt had a solid look on his face, so I couldn't read his expression.

We stood up to meet them when they reached the waiting room.

"I'm glad both of you are okay," Wyatt began, then I saw him staring at the blood on my clothes. "Alex, are you hurt?"

"No, that's not my blood," I replied quickly. "I shot one of the two gunmen, but it wasn't fatal. I was able to keep him stable until the medics arrived."

"And how's he now?" Ian asked.

"He's out of surgery. We are waiting for him to wake up so we can interrogate him," Liam answered.

I noticed a sudden change in Wyatt's expression, but it was quick, so I couldn't tell exactly what had induced it.

"Here's the file you asked for. It has all the information I could find," Ian said, handing Liam a thick file. "His name is Ronan Martinez."

Liam thanked Ian and took the file from him. It pleased me that the atmosphere between them wasn't as tense as it used to be.

"Alex, can I talk to you for a second?" Wyatt addressed me.

I nodded and started walking a little further alongside him. "What is it you needed to talk about, sir?" I asked when we were far enough from Liam and Ian so they couldn't hear us.

"Alex, you need to step off this case," he said, and my eyes widened a little.

"What? No. We are finally one step closer to the truth. Whoever was behind this failed miserably today. That man can lead us to them," I argued, my tone getting higher with every word coming out of my mouth.

"Alex, this case became so dangerous, and I can't stand still and watch the past repeating itself with you," he retorted, looking at me sternly.

I breathed heavily as the meaning behind his words was making me uneasy. "Sir, we all walk out of our homes every day, not knowing for sure if we will return home unscathed. This job is always dangerous."

Meeting his eyes evenly, I continued. "I'm really grateful for your concern, but I don't need anybody to tell me what to do with my life. I'm very capable of protecting and taking care of myself."

He scoffed. "You're so stubborn, just like your father. But watch out, Alex, that can be the end of you as it was for him. Do you think he'd be happy to see you walking down the same path that had gotten him killed?"

His words sounded more like a threat, and that made me flare with anger. I clutched my fists and breathed heavily. I was about to say something to him, but Liam approached us and interrupted me.

"Alex, he's awake," Liam told me.

"Excuse me," I said to Wyatt and didn't wait for his response as I quickly walked away, brushing past Liam, who was eying the situation carefully.

"What happened with Wyatt?" Liam asked, walking beside me.

"Never mind," I dismissed, not wanting to talk about it. I looked at the shooter's file. "Let's just focus on this son of a bitch for now."

Liam nodded, and I was thankful that he didn't press the issue.

We walked to the shooter's room. It had two officers waiting in front of it. Liam and I shared a look before he opened the door and we walked inside.

He jerked upright when he saw us, but his wrists refused to move, metal digging into his skin as both of his hands were cuffed to the bed's railing.

"Ronan Martinez, isn't it?" Liam asked, radiating an intimidating vibe.

He seemed nervous that we knew his name, even though he tried hard not to show it.

"So, who is your partner, and where can we find him?" Liam asked again, but the man remained silent.

I stepped into the picture. "Oh, it seems like you have a hard time talking, do you?" I asked, looking at him in disgust.

"Oh, let's see what we have here." I opened his file and pretended to read through it. "Hmm, interesting. It says that your wife died a year ago and that you have a little daughter. I'm wondering what's going to happen to her after you are gone," I continued, trying to push his buttons.

"My daughter stays out of this," he hissed at me.

I smirked, knowing that I had gotten under his skin. I rarely played bad cop, but I was good at it whenever I did. "Well, if you want to protect her, all you have to do is tell us everything you know about your partner and your boss," I said, crossing my arms together.

He jeered. "You don't get it, do you?" he asked, and I raised an eyebrow in return. "If I opened my mouth, I would be signing a death contract with the grim reaper."

Liam clenched his fist as he made it closer to Martinez. "And don't you realize that you have just murdered an innocent man and tried to kill two federal agents? You will be sent to a super-maximum-security prison for the rest of your life, and your daughter will be placed in a foster home. You will never see her again. I can assure you we will do everything in our power to make sure your life will be a living hell unless you cooperate."

"And I told you if I do say anything, my daughter and I will be as good as dead," Martinez told Liam.

"What if we make you a deal?" I suggested, grabbing the attention of both Martinez and Liam.

He seemed to be interested in what I said as he concentrated his gaze on me.

"You tell us what you know, and we will offer you and your daughter protection. We can get you and your daughter into the witness protection program. You'll be provided with new identities, so nobody will be able to track both of you," I said. "The Marshals will protect your daughter, and she can visit you weekly in prison."

He looked like he was running my offer in his head, but he seemed hesitant.

"Tick, Tock, we don't have the whole day here. Are you in or not?" I asked, pushing him to say something.

"Yes," he said with a defeated sigh.

"Good," I said, a little smirk on my face.

"Who was the one behind this?" Liam asked, crossing his arms.

"Seth Mancini," he muttered so quietly that we could barely hear him.

My eyes widened a fraction as I looked at Liam. We both shared a knowing look before rushing out of the room.

Martinez just provided us with everything we needed to hold Mancini accountable. And we knew we needed to catch him before he could get any chance to disapp ear...

Chapter 18

Liam and I walked into the casino where we knew Seth Mancini was present, a couple of SWAT agents accompanying us.

We finally had the needed information to charge him, and we made sure that this time, he wouldn't be able to elude our grasp.

We flashed our badges in the face of whoever stood in our way and continued to walk without being deterred until we reached Mancini's office. The SWAT members were the first to burst into the room. We followed behind them, proud smiles decorating our faces.

He instantly rose from his seat, glaring at us with a bitter expression. He narrowed his eyes when they landed on me and Liam, showing that he was indeed scorning our presence—or maybe that we were still alive.

"How dare you dash into my office like that? And what the hell do you want this time?"

Smirking, I brought out a piece of paper and showed it to him. "The last time we were here, you told us to bring a warrant the next time we visit you. Guess what? We took by your advice."

His eyes widened a fraction, and his body tensed when Liam approached him.

"Seth Mancini, you're under arrest for solicitation of murder for hire," Liam said as he slapped his handcuffs on Mancini with his hands tied behind his back. Then he started reading him the Miranda rights. "You have the right to remain silent. Anything you say can and will be used against you in a court of law. You have the right to an attorney. If you cannot afford an attorney, one will be provided for you."

He didn't resist the arrest or even uttered a word. Instead, his face was an impeccable mask.

However, he gave me—out of everyone in the room—a look I couldn't understand just before the SWAT members led him away...

***

We were now back at the bureau. Mancini was placed in a holding cell while we were gathering all the documents and information that could be used against him in the interrogation.

Arresting such a big shot like him was as magnitude as it could get, and we had to get as much information as we could out of him.

We were interrupted when an agent walked in, clearing his throat to get our attention. He had an uneasy look on his face.

"What's wrong? Did anything happen with Mancini?" Liam was the first to speak up.

"Well, yea—"

The agent tried to say, but Liam quickly interrupted him.

"What? Did he escape?" Liam queried in an urgent tone.

The agent shook his head quickly. "No, he's well-guarded and doesn't have any chance to even think about it."

I let out a breath of relief. Losing him after everything that happened would be a catastrophe.

"Then what?" Liam snapped, looking irritated.

"Um... he wants to speak with Agent Ryan. Alone," he answered, giving me a weird look, and he emphasized the word alone.

I rose an eyebrow in bewilderment. "Me?"

"Yes, he said that he will cooperate and tell us everything we need to know. But only if we let him speak to you first before his interrogation," he replied, shrugging a little.

To be honest, I was surprised, and even a little suspicious. I had no idea why on earth Mancini wanted to speak with me specifically, or what I was about to hear.

"Did he lawyer up?" I asked the agent.

He shook his head in return.

"Fine, I will speak to him," I decided, rising from my seat. If this guaranteed getting him to talk, then it was definitely worth a shot.

"Alex, this man wanted us dead just a few hours ago. You can't go in there by yourself," Liam argued, trying to talk me out of it. "And don't you find it a little odd that a man like him didn't ask for a lawyer? He's definitely got something in mind."

"He has no power in here. And if he ever decides to do anything stupid, I will make sure he regrets it. But I need to know what he has to say to me," I said with firm persistence, giving Liam a look that meant I had already made up my mind.

Liam sighed, perhaps surrendering to the fact that he wouldn't change my mind.

"Just be careful, and no matter what, don't let him get under your skin."

I nodded quickly before I walked out of the room and started making my way toward Mancini's cell.

A wicked smile started playing around the edges of Mancini's mouth When I reached his cell.

Ignoring him, I schooled my face into a calm, confident mask. There was no chance I was going to give him any chance to hold anything against me or provoke me in any way.

I gave a small nod to the guards standing in front of his cell. One of them opened the door for me and then locked it up again after I was inside.

Crossing my arms, I eyed Mancini with a stern look while keeping a little distance between us.

He smiled before starting to speak. "Maybe it's best if we could have a little privacy here."

"I'm not sure if it occurred to you or not, but you don't get to make any demands in here," I said in a dry tone, still maintaining a solid look on my face.

"You really want to listen to what I have to say." He met my eyes evenly, the smile all gone from his face.

I narrowed my eyes at him, then I gave another nod to the guards outside the cell. They left their place in front of the cell. My inner voice of reason scolded me for agreeing to be all by myself in a locked cell with the man who wanted me dead only a few hours ago. I tried my best to ignore it.

I sat on the bench in front of him, making sure to maintain enough distance between us. "Are you comfortable enough to speak now?" I studied him carefully, looking out for any reaction.

He just smiled and looked down at the tattoo on his hand—the tattoo that was identical to the one that kept haunting me for years.

"This one is called Vegvísir. It's a symbol of protection and guidance. In the old Norse, people used to carry this runic compass with them all the time, or even carve it on their bodies. They believed it protected people from getting lost by helping them choose the right path in life and guiding them through hard times."

"I'm not here to talk about tattoos," I said between gritted teeth, feeling that I was running out of patience.

"Forgive me, but I thought you would be interested in that one in particular," he said, looking at me with narrowed eyes and a ghost of a malicious smile on his face.

My eyes widened a fraction when I realized the meaning behind his words, feeling my facade slipping. I tried to hide my change of expression quickly so I wouldn't give him any chance to take control of the situation. Unfortunately, I just couldn't do the same with my trembling hands.

It was him... I was sitting right in front of the man who ripped me off my family.

My whole body stiffened as if the temperature in the cell had dropped 10 degrees all of a sudden. My heart pounded in my chest as images from that night flashed through my brain.

My mother's blood, scattered everywhere. The sound of the bullet that took my father's life. And then... the image of the man who pulled the trigger—the same man who was currently sitting right in front of me.

My blood was boiling as hot as lava in my veins. I clenched my fist so hard that my knuckles turned white. I was fighting the impulse to do something I knew I would regret later.

Closing my eyes, I reminded myself that the bastard sitting in front of me wasn't worth wasting my life. He was already going to get what he deserved.

Bitter, pregnant silence filled the atmosphere around us for a few minutes, but they seemed like a lifetime to me.

"Why?" I uttered, finally breaking the silence with the only word I was able to push out of my mouth.

"At the time, I was just following orders I couldn't say no to," he said with a shrug.

There was no sign of remorse in his callous eyes. He looked as if he had done nothing wrong.

Something deep down in my heart knew that it was him all along, but watching him admit it was a whole different scenario.

I always wondered what I would do if I ever met him—the man that haunted my worst nightmares. I wondered if I would end up his life with a shot to the head, just like he did to my father. Or if I would rip his heart out of his chest with my bare hands the same way he did to me all that time ago.

But here I was, sitting in front of him, feeling paralyzed, unable to do anything.

"I want to help you," he abruptly spoke up with seriousness in his tone.

My eyes widened a little, and I felt like laughing despite myself. The man who murdered my parents was offering to help me.

"Oh really? Did you just grow a heart all of a sudden?" I scoffed, letting out a humorless laugh. "Or do you think I'm dumb or desperate enough to accept help from a cold-blooded murderer like you?" I rose from where I was seated, unable to hold my anger in anymore.

"Look, Alex, I—"

He was about to say something, but I immediately stopped him mid-sentence. "No, you don't get to say my name with your filthy mouth," I hissed at him, feeling sickened by his mere presence.

The oxygen in the cell was getting scarcer as more time passed. I wanted to finish whatever this was as fast as I could, as I was having an inner fight with myself, trying to keep my temper in check.

"I just need you to listen to what I'm about to say. You won't regret it," he insisted.

I kept looking at him in disgust and hatred, fighting the urge to do something impulsive.

Taking a deep breath, I sat back on the bench and crossed my arms, waiting to hear what he had to say. "It better be worth it."

He let out a long sigh before he spoke. "In the world where I'm involved in head to toe, there's no place for failure, and as you see, I screwed up." He smiled bitterly and gestured to the cell we were currently in. "If you haven't already noticed, I became a burned card. I'm living on borrowed time, and my clock began its final countdown the second you caught me."

I couldn't bring myself to say anything, but I wanted him to continue, so I gave him the go on look.

"Your father was an honorable man, no doubt about it, but he never knew when to quit. He refused to give up on that case even after he got dismissed from it. He continued to work on it secretly for years, and he uncovered a lot of truths and secrets that were never supposed to see the light of day."

Hearing him mention my father made me even angrier, but I stayed silent as I wanted to see the end of what he was telling me.

He broke eye contact with me and looked away, as his mind was probably taking him on a trip down memory lane.

"He gathered lots of files and information that could incriminate dozens of noted names in this country, and all of them wanted your father dead."

I felt many pieces of the puzzle being connected in my head. Everything was indeed connected to that damn case, and it actually made sense.

But where were those files? I found nothing related to the case in my father's office except for the file that contained a few photos and some unimportant details.

"We looked everywhere for those files, but we have never found them. They're still out there somewhere, and you need to find them," he said, giving me a serious look. "You might have won one battle by arresting me, but you still have a long war ahead of you."

"Well, you could be saying the truth, and you could also be trying to get me distracted, or even drive me into an ambush. Give me one good reason why I should ever trust you," I said sternly, locking my eyes with his cold, dark ones.

"You shouldn't." He shrugged. "And actually, you shouldn't trust anybody. There are a lot of dirty people involved, even inside the walls of the mighty FBI. Someone close to your father gave him away."

Thinking about it now, he was right. If what he said was true, it would mean that my father worked on the case secretly for years. Then someone close to him must have discovered what he was doing and sold him out.

But who?

"I still have more questions," I spoke up, and he nodded. "I believe the Chinese symbol is your act of power and control. Why didn't you leave it there when you did what you did?" When you murdered my parents. But I couldn't bring myself to say it.

His lips tilted up in a small smile. "Come on, now. That would have linked a lot of puzzle pieces together, and we definitely didn't want for that to happen."

A pile rose in my throat. I was about to say something else to him but was cut off by two agents who opened the cell's metal door.

"Agent Ryan, we have to take him for interrogation now," one of them said.

I nodded at them, then I returned to give Mancini a last look. Lots of thoughts and questions were reeling through my mind.

An agent approached Mancini, cuffing him with his hands behind his back.

"As I previously mentioned, I am a dead man walking. They will get rid of me as soon as they can. But I don't care, because I have already played my last wild card. You," he told me as the agents escorted him away.

"Good luck, kid. You will need it."

I heard him shouting before he disappeared from my view.

I stood there inside of the empty cell, motionless, trying to cope with everything I just learned. And I wondered whom I could trust, and who could be a potential enemy...

***

The clock on my wall ticked like the timer of a bomb, each tick making me feel more agitated and helpless.

It wasn't the only sound in the room, though. The beating of my own heart was also as loud. It kept pounding unmercifully against its cage of bone and cartilage.

After the little talk I had with Mancini, I went straight to my apartment. And I had lost count of how many hours I have been sitting here, on the couch, buried in thought.

I still didn't know what to do with the pieces of information Mancini had given me, or even if I should believe him at all.

It crossed my mind that he might have told me all of that to get me into an ambush. He was a criminal and a cold-blooded murderer—my parents' murderer, for that matter. I still couldn't believe I managed to keep myself in check while he was sitting in front of me, showing no remorse or regret for the blood that covered his hands.

Letting out a sigh, I ran my fingers through my hair for what seemed like the millionth time, and that was only in the past hour. I was desperate, having no idea what my next move should be.

Abruptly, the doorbell snapped me out of my thoughts. I jumped like the button was hard-wired to my brain.

I wasn't expecting anybody, so I reached out for my gun and clung to it tightly behind my back. I walked slowly toward the door.

As I turned the door, I hardened my grip on the gun. But I let out a breath I didn't know I was holding when I found a pair of deep blue eyes looking straight at me.

"Alex, thank God." Liam let out a breath. "I was hoping to find you here. I looked everywhere for you after Mancini was taken for questioning, and I got worried when I didn't find you," he said.

Then his eyes narrowed when he noticed the gun in my hand. He stepped inside the apartment and closed the door behind him. "Alex, what's really going on?"

"Nothing. Everything's peachy," I said dismissively, making my way back to the living room. I sat down on the couch and put the gun on the table in front of me. I was making sure not to look him in the eye.

He followed me to the living room and took a seat next to me. "Don't you know that you're a terrible liar?"

It was true. I hated nothing more than lies, and liars for that matter, so maybe that was why I wasn't a very good one. I let out a sigh, saying nothing.

"Alex..." Liam called, forcing me to look at him. He had a dead-serious expression on his face. "Mancini was murdered while he was being transferred to prison. He and the marshals who were escorting him."

My eyes widened in shock. Mancini's words hit me. He really was telling the truth.

"Does it have anything to do with what he wanted to talk to you about?" Liam pressed, blue eyes fixed on me.

I looked at him with unsure eyes, not sure if I should tell him.

He must have noticed my hesitation, because he closed the gap between us and grabbed my hands. An electric shock radiated through my whole body.

He looked me in the eye. "Do you trust me?"

I was a little bothered by how he could read me like a book, but the answer to that question was really easy. Liam was the only one in too long to enter my life and stay. The only one I felt I could really trust, even with my biggest secret. But this wasn't only about trust, it was more about fear. Fear of what was going to happen next, of what I was going to walk into, not knowing if it would cost me my life. I didn't want to drag him into this.

However, I really didn't want to be alone either. I didn't want to find the files and fight the war all by myself. I knew it was selfish of me, but I had to be honest with myself and admit that I needed him.

I looked him in the eyes and murmured. "Yes, Liam. I trust you."

He cracked a smile. "Then you can tell me anything."

I let out another sigh before I started telling him every-thing that Mancini had told me. By the time I finished, he was having wide eyes and looked startled.

He was silent for a few moments, probably trying to comprehend everything. I knew it was a lot to take in.

"Liam, look," I spoke up, grabbing his attention. "I'm about to get into a war I barely have any chance of winning. I don't even have the weapons I can fight with yet. And I know for sure it's dangerous. I have witnessed its consequences with my own eyes, after all." I looked at my hands that were folded in my lap and fiddled a little with my fingernails. "So, I can perfectly understand if what I said might have scared you, and if you want to back off—"

"Alex, stop," Liam interrupted me before I could say anything else. I was keeping my face down, so he grabbed it and forced me to look him directly in the eye.

There was something about his eyes that always brought a sense of reassurance to my heart. Not to mention that they had the most beautiful shade of blue I had ever seen.

"We're partners. We got involved in this case together, and it's only fair if we continue together," he said. "And more importantly, I care about you, and I'm never letting you go through this all by yourself. So, I'm afraid you're stuck with me." He shrugged with a slight grin.

I couldn't help but smile.

In this life, everyone needed a harbor, an anchor to hold on to. Someone with whom we could always feel safe and secure, no matter what we were dealing with. Someone who could help us forget all the burdens of the world, even if it was only momentary.

Or else, life would become full of constant torment. And we would be simply expected to endure it all by ourselves while it devoured our souls, slowly and painfully. Until we could no longer recognize the shell of a person we were slowly turning into.

And at this very moment, I felt like I had finally found my harbor. Liam brought a feeling of safety and warmth to my life. Even at one of my scariest and most uncertain moments, he was the rock that stood firm amidst the avalanche.

"So, let's begin with something easy." His voice brought me back to reality. "Do you know anything about those files?"

I shook my head in disappointment.

He sighed and ran his fingers through his hair. "We need to find them," he said, pointing out the obvious.

"I know, but I don't even know where to look," I replied, feeling helpless. It was probably written all over my face because Liam put his hands on mine in a soft gesture.

"Alex, it's okay." He gave me a warm smile. "I'm sure we'll find something. Don't be so hard on yourself."

I nodded, giving him a small, reassuring smile. I was glad to have him right here with me. It was good to know that I wasn't alone through all this chaos.

Hours went by as we kept considering every possible place where the files could have been hidden. I was certain they weren't at our old home. They must have torn it upside down on the day of the murder, and I have found nothing useful in my father's office, either.

Letting out a sigh, I ran my fingers through my hair. A little harder than I intended as I ended up pulling out a few hairs as collateral damage, making me grimace. A wave of despair washed over me.

Where on earth could the files be?

Suddenly, something flared inside my head. I instantly rose from my seat, holstered my gun, and started fixing my hair and clothes in the mirror.

Liam remained seated, only giving me a perplexed look.

"Come on, get up," I told him. "I think I know someone who might have something useful for us."

"Who?" Liam asked, standing up.

"My grandmother," I replied, a hopeful smile on my face.

Chapter 19

I parked the car in front of my grandmother's house in the suburbs of Westchester County, where I grew up.

It occurred to me that my dad might have told her something when he suspected he was exposed. Also, I remembered that had an old room at my grandparent's house that he used as an office when he was studying at Quantico. And he spent lots of time there whenever we stayed over there. I hoped we would find some clues in there.

I rushed to the front door, Liam following behind me.

Ringing the doorbell, I noticed that my heartbeats were racing.

My grandfather passed away a few years ago, and my grandmother was currently living all by herself. That made me very guilty when I decided to move out and rent an apartment in the heart of the city so I would be close to the Federal Plaza.

However, my grandmother had already gotten used to having me away from her since my Quantico days. It helped her make peace with the fact that her baby girl and favorite granddaughter had become a grown-up woman. And of course, I had promised to visit her a lot. But with everything that happened in the past few months, I had broken that promise and was definitely about to get into so much trouble for it.

The door opened, and I was met with my grandmother's warm hazel eyes. Her worried expressions changed the moment her eyes met mine.

She hurried and pulled me in for a hug. I hugged her back tightly and buried my face in her shoulders.

I remembered when I was a little kid, and her hugs made all my worries disappear like rain on summer's earth. I really wished that could happen now, too.

She held my face in her hands when she broke the hug. "Alex, my dear. I missed you so much."

"I missed you too, Granny." I took a good look at her. She was still wearing her sleeping gown, as it was still pretty early in the morning. Liam and I stayed up all night, so we really didn't consider this little detail. "I'm really sorry for waking you up so early, and for not calling before I came here."

"Honey, you can come here anytime you want." She smiled at me, then her gaze shifted to Liam, who was standing a little farther from us.

I gestured for him to come closer. "Oh, Granny. This's Liam Hunt, my partner."

He smiled politely and extended his hand for her to shake it. "It's a pleasure to meet you, ma'am."

My grandmother ignored his extended hand and pulled him into a hug.

I chuckled when I noticed the embarrassed look that was drawn on Liam's face.

"He's such a sweetheart," my grandmother said when she broke the hug, looking at me.

I just grinned, and I could see Liam blush a little.

"And please, just call me Ellen," she told him, and he nodded quietly.

She gestured for us to get inside the house. "Come on, get in. From your faces, I could tell that there's something serious going on."

She chuckled when I raised an eyebrow at her, wondering how she knew that.

"I have raised two FBI agents. This's only natural by now."

That made both Liam and me smile.

"But whatever you got, it has to wait after breakfast," she said with a look that meant it wasn't even up for discussion.

We got in. She guided Liam toward the living room and stopped me before I had the chance to join him.

"He's definitely easy on the eyes." She grinned.

My eyes widened a little at hearing this come out of my grandmother, even though a blindfolded person could easily agree with this little fact.

"And he's my partner." I gave her a look that said what she was implying was impossible.

She shrugged. "From the way you both look at each other, I think you're more than just that." She winked at me before she disappeared into the kitchen, and left me motionless, thinking about what she had just told me.

Well, we were close friends and not just partners, but could we be even more than that?

I shook my head. That was definitely not the best time to be thinking about something like that.

I joined Liam in the living room but didn't sit down.

"Your grandmother is lovely," Liam spoke up, smiling at me.

"She is, indeed." I smiled back, thinking about the countless memories I shared with her. "She was so strong after what happened, even though she had just lost her son and her daughter-in-law. But thinking about it now, I know it was only because of me. She tried so hard to fill the void that day left in me. She was the solid rock I leaned on and kept me from falling apart, and she knew that very well."

Liam gave me a compassionate look but remained silent.

"Come on, let's check the office upstairs." I have already told Liam about my dad's old office on our way here.

He nodded and followed me upstairs. We went into the office, and it looked like it had been used yesterday. I remembered my grandmother used to spend a lot of time here, after what happened, and probably to this very day.

We started looking everywhere, but there were only files of old cases and books from his student days. There were also a couple of boxes that were stuffed with papers and files. Liam and I started looking through them thoroughly.

We found a file that had the word confidential printed on the cover; we opened it quickly. It contained many pictures of murder victims, identical to the ones I had found before. The infamous Chinese symbol was the common factor in every murder case in those files.

There were also pictures of some people, but we didn't know any of them. Besides, most of the information in the papers was sealed, so we couldn't find anything useful.

"This can't be what Mancini was talking about," I said, looking at the file in my hand in disappointment. "It has nothing."

I slammed the file on the desk in anger, and when I did, a small note fell from it. I kneeled and picked it up and looked at it carefully. It was definitely written in my dad's handwriting.

"What's written on it?" Liam asked.

I showed it to him. The note only had the name Peter Harris, and the letters NYPD written next to it.

"Alex, this could be a lead," Liam said, his blue eyes lighting up.

I nodded, looking at the note again. We had to find this Peter Harris.

"Breakfast's ready," my grandmother called from downstairs.

We decided to make do with what we got, and we went downstairs to join my grandmother. From the smell, I could tell that she had prepared my favorite breakfast, and I grinned when I found out that I was right.

As we ate breakfast together, we talked about many random things, and it felt good for a while, but I knew I had to tell her about the case inevitably. However, I kept wondering how I was going to open up the subject with her.

How was I supposed to tell her that I was currently working on the same case that got her son killed? Not only that, but I was also about to walk down the same path he took.

I finished my coffee, and when I finally felt that the caffeine had started to kick in, I decided it was about time to tell her why we were actually here.

"Granny," I addressed her.

"Getting down to business, I see." She smiled. "What's wrong, Honey?"

"I—I wanted to ask you if Dad mentioned keeping any files away, or if he had secret places anywhere, especially before he um—" I paused. I couldn't bring myself to continue, but I knew I didn't need to from the look on her face.

Rubbing my hands, I let out a deep breath to regain control and looked at Liam, who gave me a reassuring look.

I watched as my grandmother closed her eyes, looking in deep thought for a few moments. Then she shook her head.

"I don't think he had ever told me about anything like this. But why are you looking for them now?" she asked, and I could see her eyes clouding with apprehension.

I opened my mouth a few times, but no words came out of it. I looked at Liam for rescue.

"We're currently working on a case, and we think the files in question might be of great help," Liam answered her question, taking in my silent SOS signal.

"A case?" she asked, then she looked at me once again. "Alex, don't tell me it's related to—" She paused, but I knew exactly what she meant. "To whatever got your father killed." She was now looking at me with pleading eyes.

I remained silent for a few moments, thinking about the right words to use. Then I sighed and closed my eyes. "It is," I admitted.

"Alex, are you out of your mind?" she yelled, and I could see the tears already gathering in her eyes.

"Grandma, we got the man who did it," I told her, thinking it might bring her peace if she knew that.

"I don't care. It has been too many years for that wound to be ripped open again and for you to give up your life for it."

A few tears rolled down her cheeks, and it broke my heart to see her like this.

"Alex, I can't lose you too." She shook her head, her voice breaking.

I walked up to her and kneeled down on the floor. I wiped the tears from her face with a gentle touch.

"You will not lose me. I promise you I will be okay. I will win this war and come back to you," I told her, feeling the tears already burning in my eyes. "But you need to understand. Dad worked so hard to gather the information within those files because he knew how important they were. They will help bring down so many bad people. So, it's my duty toward him, toward my job, and toward the oath I took, to find them and bring them to light."

She wiped her tears and nodded. "I understand." Then she looked at Liam, who was watching all of this in silence. "Please, take good care of her."

I noticed that Liam was caught off-guard, but he nodded quickly. "I will," he said, and from the look in his eyes, I knew he meant it.

I hugged my grandmother one last time and promised her again that I would be okay, then Liam and I left the house.

Now, we had one goal, and it was to find out everything there was to find on Peter Harris...

***

Peter Harris was a retired cop who used to work at the NYPD. We also discovered that he was assigned to that same case for a while. However, there wasn't much accessible information about him at that time, and he spent little time working on it either.

But the weirdest part was that he retired only a few weeks after my parents were killed, which made us confident that he knew something.

He was currently living with his family in Queens, and that was where we were headed, knowing there was no time to waste. We were desperate for any leads.

Liam finally parked the car in front of a family house. We got out and rang the doorbell.

A middle-aged man opened the door. A dazed expression dominated his features. He had tanned skin, and a thin, high-cheeked face, with many vertical wrinkles. His dark brown eyes stared at us.

I knew the look in them—it told me they were filled with obvious pain and hidden trauma.

"Can I help you?" he asked, looking at us warily.

Liam and I got out our badges and showed them to him.

"Sir, we were wondering if we could get to ask you a few questions?" Liam was the first to respond.

The man looked as if he didn't hear what Liam said. He kept his gaze fixed on my badge, and on me.

"Alexandra!" he murmured quietly, almost to himself.

"You know me?" I questioned, feeling a thin thread of hope creeping into me. Nonetheless, I received no answer to my question.

"Sorry, I can't help you," the man blurted out.

My eyes widened, taken aback by his reaction.

He was about to close the door, but Liam put his leg in the way and stopped him.

"Sir, please," Liam said. "We just need to speak to you for a while."

The man never took his eyes off me. He was silent for a couple of minutes, looking like he was in a debate with himself. He finally sighed, giving in, as he gestured to the inside of the house.

We went in and as soon as we were all seated in the living room. I decided to start, as several questions were burning on my tongue.

"Sir, we're here because—"

"I know why you're here," he spoke, cutting me off. "And yes, I know you." He was studying me with a soft expression on his face.

Liam and I shared a look, but we remained silent and waited for him to continue.

"Your father was one of my best friends. We met when we were working together on the case of the Chinese symbol. Isn't that why you're here, Alex?" he asked.

I nodded quickly, feeling my heart racing in my chest.

He let out a sigh. "Your father and I both shared the same level of interest in that case. We knew that there were many fishy secrets behind it, and we wanted to find them."

He looked distant, as if he was remembering the old days. "Even after we both got dismissed from the case, we continued to work on it secretly for years. We uncovered lots of dirt that would have incriminated lots of vicious people and big-shots in the country."

Mancini's words started hitting me again, and I hoped that he would have any information that would lead us to the files.

"We were finally ready to bring all we found to light, but around that time, your father noticed he was being watched. He discovered that someone really close to him was, in fact, a mole. Someone in the FBI." He paused a little and took a deep breath before he continued. "Your father was sensing danger from all around. He wanted to get you and your mother somewhere safe. He said he would die if anything happened to you, but... it was already too late."

My chest tightened, and I felt a lump in my throat. I thought Liam might have noticed because he closed the gap between us and put a reassuring hand on mine.

"Everything happened too fast. I—I was shell-shocked when I heard about what happened, and I didn't know what to do," he said, looking at the ground.

"I thought they had gotten their hands on the files. But a few days after your father was—" He paused, raising a shaky hand to wipe the sweat that had formed on his forehead. "I—I received a box that contained everything with a letter from your father, asking me to do the right thing."

His eyes were teary as he continued. "I couldn't do it. I—I was scared. So, I left my job and went off the ground for a while until I made sure they weren't looking for me. But I couldn't get rid of the files, and I lived with that guilt all my life. You need to understand, I had a family too, and I wasn't as bold as your father was." He looked at me with pleading eyes.

"I understand that very well," I assured him. "But do you happen to still have those files?" I asked, silently praying to hear a positive reply.

He nodded before he slowly rose from his seat and disappeared upstairs.

The ticking of the clock on the wall seemed as if it were in sync with my heartbeats. They were both the only audible sounds in the room. I felt like I was holding my breath and wasn't able to let it out.

Liam squeezed my hand tightly, but said nothing. I guessed he might have been feeling the same.

After another few torturing minutes, Peter Harris came back to the living room, a box in his hand.

He put the box on the table in front of us and handed me the files. "You need to be really careful with those and think twice before trusting anybody."

I nodded as I took the files from him, staring at them in disbelief. A part of me still couldn't believe we finally got our hands on them.

"James would have been really proud of you, you know. Good luck, Alex," he said, bringing my attention to him.

"Thank you," I muttered as I stood up.

Liam joined me. We left the house and got back into the car, but Liam didn't start the engine.

We both sat there in silence, looking at the files, not daring to touch them yet.

Liam sighed. "We need to think clearly so we can pull this trigger at the right time," he said, pointing at the files.

I nodded. "But we need to know what's inside of them, first," I said. "Let's get back home."

Liam nodded as he turned the key and brought the car to life. Then he started driving toward my apartment.

When we arrived there, each of us grabbed a file and started reading through it. We kept reading file after file without stopping.

Hours passed, and we were still reading through the files. The information inside of them was crucial. I couldn't believe the amount of infamous, corrupt names inside of them.

Finally, I put my hand on an FBI file. "Liam, look. This may be about the mole Harris was talking about," I said, showing him the file.

He left the one that was in his hand and came closer to me. "Come on, open it," he encouraged.

Taking a deep breath, I opened the file. We both started reading through it until we finally got to a very familiar name.

We both froze, and I felt my blood turn cold.

Liam looked up and met my wide gaze.

It was no one but Wyatt...

Chapter 20

Wyatt.

I closed my eyes, hoping that they were playing some sick trick on me, but when I opened them again, his name was still there.

My mind was refusing to adapt to the fact that it was him all along. The one behind everything, the one who took my parents from me.

He was my father's friend—they were partners. My father welcomed him into our home and our family. He sat with us at the same dining table. He betrayed every ounce of friendship and morality—he was an animal. No, animals were loyal to one another, and they never turned on their own, even the wild ones. He was a monster.

I could feel the blood boiling in my veins as rage hissed through my body like a deadly poison, and hate welled up in my heart.

Standing up, I started pacing around the apartment. I was utterly disgusted.

I never believed in vengeance and retaliation, but I wanted to see him suffer, and I hated him even more for bringing out the worst version of myself.

"Alex."

I heard Liam calling my name. It was the first time he opened his mouth since we read the file. My face was red with suppressed rage, so I avoided looking at him.

"Please, don't let fury control you or it will drive you to do something you will definitely regret for the rest of your life. We need to give this a serious thought so we could reach a reasonable solution together." He emphasized the word together as he finished.

He was right. I couldn't take matters into my own hands because if I did, I would be just confusing justice with vengeance, and that wasn't me. I was a federal agent; it was my duty to restore order and not further chaos.

I took a deep breath, trying to put out the fire that was still blazing inside of me.

"What do you think we should do?" I asked, finally looking at Liam.

"We should take this to Aaron McCoy," he replied, pointing at the files.

I was about to argue with him that we couldn't trust anybody at this point, but he stopped me before I could utter a word.

"He's known to be a man of honor, and he himself exposed lots of corrupt names through the course of his career in the bureau. I really think we can trust him."

I was running what he said through my mind. I knew it was a risk, but I also knew that we needed help. It was going to be a protracted war, and it needed a hell of a lot more than just me and Liam. Plus, we couldn't just go rogue and turn our backs on the FBI just because someone was crooked.

I finally nodded, hoping that by this, we weren't actually digging our own graves...

***

It was almost midnight, but we couldn't wait until the morning. We called McCoy, who thought that we were unquestionably out of our goddamned minds for calling him at such a late hour.

However, we managed to convince him that what we had was of crucial importance, and it was absolutely worth a midnight call. Then finally, he agreed to meet us at his place.

We arrived at his home an hour later, and he led us to his home office so we could have some privacy.

"So, what do you think is so important that it couldn't wait until the morning?" McCoy questioned, clasping his hands as he looked at us with tired eyes.

Liam and I shared a nervous look, not knowing where to start.

I took a deep breath before I focused my gaze on McCoy. "Sir, I'm certain that you have heard about the conversation I had with Seth Mancini only a few hours before he was assassinated," I said knowingly.

He nodded his head, clearly showing more interest in our conversation.

"Well, he confessed to being one of the people who were involved in the murder of my parents," I told him. And I saw his eyes widen as he observed what I said.

I continued quickly before he could get the chance to make any comment. "He told me that my father worked on that case covertly for years, and he uncovered a lot of secrets, but the mob found out so they got rid of him before he could bring them out."

McCoy looked like he was having a hard time grasping everything I was telling him.

I shared a look with Liam, who gave me a supportive nod.

Bringing the files out of a briefcase we had with us, I handed them to him. He accepted them without saying anything.

"I didn't believe him at first, but then I found those," I said.

He put on his reading glasses and started looking through them. We waited impatiently as he went through most of the files.

He finally looked at us with wide eyes. "Unbelievable! We worked on this case for so many years. These files could have changed everything. I'm glad you both decided to come to me; we need to move fast."

He was about to dial a number on his landline phone, but I stopped him quickly.

"Sir, Mancini also told me that there was a mole inside the bureau—a corrupt agent."

He looked at me skeptically, so I leaned forward and handed him the one file that had Wyatt's name inside of it.

He frowned as he went through most of the file, then his eyes widened in shock before they met ours. "T—This can't be true. I trusted that man. I gave him his position, and I was even vouching for him to be my successor." He scoffed. Then he took off his glasses and gave us a determined look. "I will make sure that bastard ends up behind bars myself."

"Sir, I think we should wait," I spoke up, gaining both the attention of the director and Liam, who shot me a wary look, probably hating whatever was going on in my mind before he even heard it.

"Those files lacked one thing, the name of the mob's boss. So, if we arrest Wyatt now and reveal the files, we still won't be able to determine the identity of the upper hand in the mob. I'm sure he will find a way to rise again after we strike, and everything we do will go to waste."

"Then what do you think we should we do?" McCoy asked impatiently.

Taking a deep breath, I started telling them about the plan that was forming in my head.

***

I was walking unusually slowly. The rhythm of heart-beats increased with every step I took until I was facing a door. I knocked on it twice. I heard a rough "come in."

I took a deep breath and plastered the most deceiving smile before I walked in.

"Sir, I hope you have got some free time. There's something I need to talk to you about," I said.

"Sure, take a seat," Wyatt said with a smile that sent chills through my body.

I ignored the thoughts going on in my mind, urging me to wipe that damn smile off.

I sat down and looked him in the face. Disgust and anger were starting to boil inside me again. I took a deep breath and tried to concentrate on the mission at hand.

"I spoke to Mancini about the murder of my parents," I told him and watched as his eyes widened. I could see his body tensing.

"And then, I found those." I put the files on his desk, excluding the ones about him. Of course, they were all copies.

He wiped the sweat that was forming on his forehead as he started reading through the files. I could see that he was startled.

"W—Where did you find all of that?" he asked.

It must have been killing him to know where the files they looked for desperately for years were securely hidden all these years.

"It doesn't matter," I said dismissively, and then continued quickly. "Anyway, I didn't really know what to do, and you're the only one I trust here, so I decided to come to you for help." I tried to look desperate.

I watched as he let out a breath. "Alex, listen," he started, looking at me with obvious fake concern. "You need to back off. This's so dangerous." He pointed at the files. "Leave them with me, and I will figure out what to do with them."

I nodded. "Thank you, sir. I wouldn't know what to do without you," I said, sending him a fake smile.

"Don't worry. I won't let what your father did go to waste." He gave me a bitter smile that made me feel like throwing up.

I forced another smile before I quickly left his office and made my way to the conference room, where McCoy had already gathered the people he trusted the most.

"Were you able to plant the bug?" McCoy asked as soon as I entered the room.

I nodded as I took a seat next to Liam.

McCoy gave a nod to an analyst who started working on his computer.

There was silence for a couple of minutes, but then we heard Wyatt dialing a number on his phone. We waited to hear what he was about to say.

"I have something very precious to you; something you have been desperately wanting for too long."

His malicious smile popped up in my head as I kept listening. Unfortunately, though, we couldn't hear what the person on the other end of the line was saying.

"Fine, but you have to know that the price is going to be massive," Wyatt muttered. "Oh, and apparently, you got a problem with another Ryan. The girl knows too much. You better get rid of her sooner than later."

I clenched my fists so hard that my knuckles turned white. I really couldn't wait to make him pay for all he did.

After his phone call, Wyatt left his office, and we knew for sure that he was going to meet up with the boss. Everybody rushed outside of the conference room to make all the preparations required for the raid.

My plan worked smoothly. I was positive that Wyatt would try to get the files to the big head of the mob, and we were going to follow him and storm the meeting place.

We were now all getting ready. I was putting on my bulletproof vest when I noticed McCoy approaching me.

"Alex, can I talk to you for a minute?"

He already had his bulletproof vest on, and he was wearing an FBI windbreaker. His face was unreadable.

I nodded. "Of course, sir."

"Your father and I weren't close, but we have worked together occasionally in the past. He was a man of honor, I knew that. I always respected him, and he for sure died a hero," he said, softly. "I just want you to know that vengeance is a poison to the soul. You can't let it control you."

I gave him a little smile to assure him. "You don't need to worry about that, sir. I'm not seeking revenge; I only want justice."

He smiled. "I trust that you will do the right thing." He patted me on the shoulder before he walked away.

I noticed that Liam was watching from afar. He approached me after McCoy disappeared.

"Are you ready to watch this whole case come to an end, once and for all?" he asked.

"Honestly, I'm not even sure if this's going to help me have the closure I always yearned for."

"Alex, you should be proud that you made it to this point. You're going to fulfill what your father fought and died for."

"We. We made it to this point—together," I corrected, giving him a passionate smile.

He gave me his trademark lopsided smile that was nothing short of dazzling.

"Anyway, let's not get ahead of ourselves. We still don't know what this day holds for us." I shrugged, then I smirked at him. "But if things work out pretty well, you will owe me a shot of tequila."

Liam chuckled. "That's going to be my pleasure."

One agent came into view and said that it was time to leave. We both started walking alongside each other, but Liam abruptly stopped and stepped in front of me.

The second thing I knew was that his lips were pressed against my own and that nearly knocked all the air from my lungs.

The warmth spread from his lips throughout my whole body as the world started to fade away.

Unfortunately, Liam pulled away quickly. Probably so no one would walk on us and see what was happening, but I wished that he never did.

We stared at each other for a while, without uttering a word. But then Liam's lips twitched into a smile.

"That was for good luck," he told me before walking out of the room, leaving me there, speechless.

Blinking a few times, I tried to reconnect with the real world and make sense of what had happened.

I touched my lips and smiled.

For good luck, then.

Chapter 21

We followed Wyatt to a mansion that was a few miles outside the city.

Everything went horribly fast. We wasted no time surrounding the entire mansion and covering every possible exit.

Almost immediately, gunshots and the clanging of gun shells hitting the floor cracked into the air as loud as thunder. The count of dead bodies kept increasing as more minutes passed, leaving casualties from both sides.

Gradually, the amounts of armed men attacking us decreased. The rest of them backed down into the inside of the mansion, probably to protect their boss or escape through some hidden passageway.

We decided it was our best chance to storm in. The SWAT team was the first to dash in; we followed behind.

The place was full of dead bodies and blood portraying its many shades of red. We walked past multiple corpses as we made our way to the inside of the mansion. It was oddly quiet and empty.

They must have been trying to find a way out, but all their attempts were going to be in vain. There was an entire force already waiting for them on the outside, and there was no way they could make it out without being caught. Nonetheless, we still had to search every corner of the mansion, and we decided it was better if we separated.

Walking carefully through the corridor, I kept a firm grip on my gun as I watched out for any danger that might come from any of my four sides.

Suddenly, I heard muffled noises coming out of a room at the end of the long corridor.

Holding my breath, I reached for the doorknob. I opened the door and trudged into the room, my gun raised.

The room was pitch black, as if covered in a velvet curtain. I tried to find any source of light. But abruptly, someone shoved me down a few stairs, knocking the gun out of my hand.

I landed mercilessly on the cold ground. I had no time to process what had happened. Someone had turned the lights on, and I found myself facing a gun barrel that was pointed directly at my head.

My eyes locked with a cold, relentless gaze. The man holding the gun threw a venomous smile my way.

"I tried to warn you a lot of times, Alex, but you didn't listen. What can I say? Like father, like daughter." Wyatt scoffed, his tone vile and gruff.

"It's over, Wyatt. You won't walk out of this. The place is fully surrounded," I seethed at him, rising to my feet. His gun rose with me.

He smirked mischievously. "See, I happen to disagree with you. I have my ways, and I will get myself out of here unscathed. But sadly, I can't say the same about you. I'm afraid you won't live to see the light of another day."

There was a blazing fire burning inside of me, and his words were like gasoline poured on it.

I clenched my fists. "Why? Why did you do that to someone you once called a friend?" There was a part of me that needed to know why he did it.

He let out a sarcastic snicker. "Alexandra, my dear. This world doesn't understand the meaning of friendship or loyalty. There are only two kinds of people in this world: predator and prey. It's your choice to be either the hunter or the prey." A wicked smile was drawn on his face as he shrugged. "I just chose to be the former."

His words blinded me with a five-course rage that tasted bitter. "Then you should really beware, because every predator is somebody else's prey."

Before he could even know what was happening, I scuttled toward him, and my fist came in contact with his face. Then, I threw a kick at him that caused him to fall to the ground, wailing in pain.

He started shooting his gun aimlessly. I managed to dodge most of the bullets, but suddenly, I felt a throbbing pain in the upper part of my left arm, causing me to lose my balance. Blood oozed thickly and soaked my shirt.

Putting my hand on the wound, I looked at Wyatt, who had taken the opportunity and was now back on his feet.

He pointed the gun back again at me and smiled. "Any last words, Ryan?"

"I hope you burn in hell," I said, clenching my teeth.

I wasn't scared of him—or death, for that matter. I stopped fearing it since that day. Instead, it made me wonder if I would ever reunite with my parents in the afterlife.

"I don't think so." He smirked, putting his finger on the trigger, squeezing it slowly.

Closing my eyes, I waited to hear the sound of the bullet that would put everything to an end... but it never came.

Opening my eyes, I found Wyatt trying to pull the trigger in futility. Every time he did, he was met with a click sound instead of bullets.

He had emptied his clip...

Wasting no time, a sound of both a cry and a growl erupted from me as I threw myself at him. I slammed him against the wall and connected my fist wherever I could reach.

He dropped to the ground, and there was blood coming out of his mouth and nose. He gazed at something on the floor, and he tried to reach for it. It was my gun.

I threw another kick at him that made him crawl in pain, then I hurried and picked up my gun. I pointed it at him, panting as my heart raced in my chest.

He looked at me and let out a bitter laugh, revealing teeth filled with blood. "Come on. Pull the trigger, Alex. Shoot me. Isn't this what you want?"

My hands were clasping the gun. I pulled the trigger back slowly, as if squeezing the life out of it. All while toying with the point at which a bullet might or might not be released mercilessly into the air.

There was a burning desire inside of me to pull the trigger, but I knew I couldn't let vengeance take control over me. I heard my father's voice inside my head, urging me to do the right thing.

Lowering the gun, I looked him in the eye. "No, that would just make me no better than you, and I refuse to let that happen. An eye for an eye will just cause more blindness."

I put my gun back in its holster and brought out my handcuffs. "It's over, Wyatt," I said, as I slapped the handcuffs on his wrists.

"This's not the end, Ryan," he hissed at me as I pushed him to his feet.

"I doubt so." I harshly grabbed him by the bicep and led him out of the room.

***

After that, I handed Wyatt to a SWAT agent who read him his rights and started frisking him while I was taken to an ambulance to get my gun wound treated.

"You may feel a little pain," the paramedic told me, ready to stitch the wound.

I gave him a little nod, and he started doing his job. I grimaced in pain once the needle pierced through my skin, but then I adjusted to the tingling.

A while later, I noticed Liam approaching me.

"Is it bad?" he asked, looking at my now bandaged arm, his blue eyes full of genuine concern.

"It's just a scratch," I assured him, a smile on my face. "I will live, don't worry."

He returned the smile. "Good, because I still owe you a shot of tequila. And it would have been very rude if you died and left me hanging here."

A small laugh escaped my lips, and I locked eyes with him. I haven't yet explained what happened between us before the raid, but there was one thing I was sure about. It made me happy.

When our lips connected, there was a strange feeling that stretched throughout my body. It was overwhelming, yet it made me feel complete. I wasn't used to those kinds of feelings. I didn't even remember a time when I felt such an absolute feeling.

Liam had been my backbone through all the chaos. I didn't even think that I could have done anything if he wasn't there to push me forward, to have my back. I had this strange, even frightening feeling toward him I couldn't put into words, but I knew for sure I wanted him in my life. No, the right words were, I needed him in my life.

I didn't notice that I was staring too long at him, but his blue eyes were also looking straight at me, and his dazzling smile never wavered.

"So," he broke the silence. "We have their boss in custody, as well as Wyatt. It's a huge win, Alex. We should be proud. We made it to the end and broke the case."

"Yeah," I murmured with a smile. I couldn't believe it was really over, that I had just fulfilled what I wanted all my life. To find whoever murdered my parents and make them pay. To finally have justice.

"I think we should head back to the bureau and see how the interrogation goes," Liam said. "Then we are going to enjoy our promised shot of tequila while celebrating the well-deserved victory." He smirked, offering me his hand.

Grinning, I took his outstretched hand and rose to my feet.

***

Aaron McCoy insisted that he would interrogate Wyatt himself. He promised he would make him pay for all his crimes. And he was true to his word. We charged Wyatt with a dozen different crimes, ranging from money laundering to murder. It assured me that he would be thrown into the darkest of holes and would never see the light of day ever again.

After the long interrogation was over, we watched as Wyatt was being escorted by the Marshals to the place where he belonged. The one he would spend the rest of his life behind its bars.

I gave him a victorious smile as he walked past me. His vicious eyes locked with mine, and I couldn't understand the look he was giving me.

The smile was now wiped off my face. I kept my eyes on him as he walked with the Marshals. I felt a knot forming in my stomach.

Something didn't feel right...

Out of nowhere, the entire floor started fuzzing. Everything happened so quickly, yet it felt to me like it was in slow-motion.

Wyatt snatched a gun from one of the Marshals who were escorting him and quickly pointed it in my direction.

A gunshot was fired. The noise reverberated in my ear.

I froze and waited for it to pierce through my heart, but for some reason, it didn't...

Instead, I only heard screams—familiar screams of my name.

I looked to see that Wyatt was now knocked to the ground, lying in his own pool of blood after receiving a shot from one of the many agents surrounding him.

Something was still not right, I reminded myself. I needed to focus...

Why didn't the bullet reach me? I saw it flying toward me. It should have hit me. That wasn't how it was supposed to go.

Then I realized I was covered in blood, but it wasn't mine.

I was supposed to take that bullet, not the other way around.

It wasn't supposed to be him...

Liam collapsed to the floor, fighting for breath.

I fell to the ground with him, holding him in my arms while trying to stop the bleeding as much as I could.

"No, no! Liam, stay with me," I shouted, now back to the shocking reality.

"A—Alex, I—" he tried to say something, but his mouth refused to cooperate.

No, I couldn't take in another loss. I couldn't...

"Liam, please, don't you dare close your eyes on me," I pleaded, the tears burning in my eyes, but it wasn't of any use.

I watched helplessly as the blue in his eyes faded slowly until he finally closed them.

The place was filled with chaos and people were shouting "agent down," all around me. But at this point, all I could hear was silence.

Only dead silence...

Chapter 22

"**N**o pulse," one of the many doctors surrounding him said. "I'll start CPR."

I was no longer trapped...

He started doing chest compressions. I looked at the monitor, begging it to give a pulse, a proof of life instead of the deafening sound of the flat line.

"Charge to two hundred," the doctor ordered.

"Ma'am, you need to step away," a nurse spoke to me. She probably had to repeat it a few times before I finally looked at her.

I took a few steps back, saying nothing. I didn't dare to take my eyes off him as I kept hoping that what I was experiencing right now wasn't true, only a horrible nightmare.

"Everybody clear!" the doctor yelled. Everybody stepped away from the bed. He took the paddles and placed them on Liam's chest.

"Clear," he said again. The shock was delivered. His body vibrated and rose for a second.

I looked at the monitor again, hoping to see the slightest of pulses. Anything that would mean he was still here, fighting, but there was nothing but the damn flat line.

This couldn't be happening...

I always thought that what happened to me in my childhood made me stronger and maybe even immune to all the destruction that loss caused to the souls of the living. But oh boy, I was mistaken.

With every second passing by, I felt myself shattering piece by piece, and nobody would ever put those pieces together again.

I was supposed to be in his place—I wished I was in his place. I wished he had never saved me, so I wouldn't be going through this. What would make my life worth living if he wasn't a part of it?

"Charge to three hundred," the doctor said again. One nurse nodded, and the doctor placed the paddles on top of Liam's bare chest again. "Clear," he said and delivered the shock.

Nothing happened. The monitor kept flatlining.

I could feel the fear in my chest waiting to take over. There was a tightness in my throat as I felt the air being knocked out of my lungs, but I refused to believe it was over. I couldn't lose him.

I remembered the first time we met—the fight we had. How I had despised him and wanted to give him a good punch in the face, and how I came to realize what an amazing person he was. He was kind and sincere. He never judged me, and he was always there whenever I needed him.

Being with him made me feel safe and happy. His existence in my life gave it meaning, and I was the best version of myself when I was with him. I loved him because he was there for me when I couldn't be there for myself. It was fascinating how your feelings for someone could change over time. He meant so much to me, and I would never handle losing him.

I took a few steps closer to the bed and ignored the shouts of the doctors and nurses.

I leaned closer to him and whispered in his ear. "Come on, Liam. Show them how strong you are. I know you never give up without a fight, so please fight. For me."

For some reason, I believed he was still in there and that he could hear me. I stepped back again to let the doctors do their work.

The doctor gave me a compassionate look before he said. "Come on, let's do it one more time. Charge to three hundred sixty." He put the paddles on Liam's chest once more. "Clear." He shocked Liam's body.

The procedure took seconds, but it felt like a lifetime.

I looked at the monitor and my heart leaped when I saw a little pulse on the screen, and there was a beep sound coming out of the machine.

He was there. He was still hanging there, fighting for life.

"We got a pulse," the doctor yelled. "We need to take him to the OR. Now!" They rushed and started prepping him to take him to the operating room.

After they were gone, I sat on the floor with my back rested on the wall. I felt as if I had just regained the ability to breathe again, and finally, I dared to hope...

***

It had been three hours since they took Liam to the operating room.

With every second passing, I was dying inside. And everything around me in the hospital agitated me.

The smell of antiseptics filled my nostrils, making me sick. The constant boring TV commercials and the banging of the receptionist's fingers on the keyboard were driving me insane.

I wanted to know how he was doing. I wanted to know if he was going to be okay.

Many people passed by to check on him. Ava, Caleb, and even McCoy. But they all had to leave because things were still hectic at the bureau after Wyatt's death and what he did.

Remembering Wyatt brought back the fires of fury and hatred that smoldered deep in my system. And on top of that, the feeling of guilt weighed down on my chest. I couldn't get rid of the thought that it was supposed to be me on the operating table and not Liam.

I found myself biting on my lip, but I stopped when I felt the metallic taste of blood in my mouth. I let out a sigh and looked at the clock again, and I could swear that it went backward by five minutes.

"Here."

I heard a familiar voice. I looked up to see Ian offering me a cup of coffee.

My eyes were wide. I was a little surprised by his presence.

"Thank you," I mumbled, taking the coffee from him. "What are you doing here?"

"I just thought you could use the company." He smiled, taking a seat beside me.

I managed to send him a little smile.

"How's he doing?"

"He's been in surgery for three hours now. Your guess is as good as mine," I said, drawing circles on top of the cup in my hand.

"How about you?"

I didn't know what to say, because honestly, I was a wreck.

He sighed when he didn't receive an answer. "I know this must be really hard for you, but keep holding on to hope. He will be okay."

"Yeah," I said with a slight nod, hoping it would be true.

Ian looked at me, then he let out a little laugh.

I looked at him with a raised eyebrow.

"Sorry, it's just..." he started. "I have really wanted to buy you a cup of coffee for too long, but I never expected it to be under such circumstances."

I frowned, looking at him like he was insane.

His lips twitched into a smirk. "Yes, I've wanted to ask you out and get to know you better, but I realized I had a really tough competition."

I slightly smiled. "I do not know what you are talking about," I said knowingly, avoiding looking him in the eye.

"Come on, Alex. Everybody knows you both are into each other," he said, giving me a look that probably meant it was probably the most obvious thing in the world.

I was about to argue with him, but I noticed Liam's surgeon approaching us. I instantly stood up to meet him.

Focusing on his expression, I let out a breath of relief when I saw that he looked relaxed, and I thought he even had a ghost of a smile on his lips.

"I'm glad to inform you that the surgery was successful. We removed the bullet and stopped the bleeding," he said. "However, we had to remove the spleen. But don't worry, it's no big deal. People can have a perfectly normal life without it.

"We expect Mr. Hunt to make a full recovery with no major complications."

I felt like I was holding all the world's weight on my shoulders and finally could get it all off.

A slow smile made its way to my lips. "Thank you, Doctor," I said gratefully. "When will I be able to see him?"

"He's still under anesthesia, and it's going to be a while till he wakes up. But you can wait in the room with him if you want," he replied, smiling.

I thanked him once more before he left.

"Well, it looks like my job here is done," Ian said. "I'm really glad he's okay."

"Thank you, Ian." I gave him a little smile. "Thank you for being here. It meant a lot to me."

"Anytime." He smiled. "Well, maybe I can buy you a cup of coffee another time. But don't worry, it's only going to be a token of friendship."

I chuckled. "I will take that into consideration."

Ian sent me another smile I knew was genuine. "It was a pleasure working with you. Both of you, actually."

I gave him a gentle hug before he left, then a nurse took me to Liam's room.

He was still unconscious, but he looked much better than he did three hours ago. A little color had returned to his face, and he no longer needed a ventilator to breathe for him. He was lying peacefully beneath the sheets. I watched as his chest rose and fell with each steady breath.

I let out a little smile before I took a seat next to his bed. My eyes wandered to his heart monitor. The beeping sound of his heartbeat was soothing. It gave me the reassurance that his heart was still beating, and that he was there, holding on to life.

An hour passed. I kept watching him carefully and checking his heart monitor every once in a while, terrified that something could go wrong.

I stood up to pour myself a cup of water, but I almost dropped the glass to the ground when I heard a faint voice.

"A—Alex," Liam called, his voice raspy and a bit unclear.

I rushed to his bed. "Hey, you," I said. The smile on my face was so huge that it brought a little pain to the corners of my mouth.

"Hey." A little, lopsided smile was drawn on his face.

"You shouldn't have done that, Liam," I said, reaching out to hold his hand. "That bullet wasn't meant for you."

He squeezed my hands as tightly as he could and focused his tired blue eyes on me. "I would have never forgiven myself if I had let anything happen to you. At that moment, nothing else mattered, Alex. Nothing but you." His lips twitched into a gorgeous smile. "Besides, I have promised your grandmother to keep you safe, remember?"

I let out a chuckle and tried to push away the tears that were gathering in my eyes. "You know, I'm kind of really into people who tend to keep their promises."

He smirked. "Speaking of promises. I believe I still owe you a shot of tequila."

I grinned. "Yeah, you do. And it would have been really awful if you have died on me and just left me hanging here," I teased, remembering the similar words he had said to me. "That would have driven me mad, and I warn you, I'm quite scary when I get mad."

He let out a quiet laugh, and it sounded like a melody to my ears.

"I will make sure to never do that in the future," he said, then the left side of his lips tugged upward into the smirk that always gave me inner delight. "You know, now would be a great time to have our second kiss. But you know I just had surgery, and my mouth must smell awful."

I let out a laugh before I leaned forward and placed my lips on his. It was slow, soft, and comforting in ways that words could never express. I could feel the endorphin rushing in my body, and there was a pleasant euphoric warmth.

"That was for good luck," I whispered to him when we broke the kiss.

He gave me a huge grin before he pressed his lips against mine again. And slowly, the world started to fade away, together with all the troubles and hassles of that long day.

***

A few weeks later:

I looked at the gravestones in front of me with a smile.

It was the first time I visited my parents' graves and felt good about it. I felt that they finally could rest in peace, knowing they didn't die in vain and that what my father did would never be forgotten.

Liam approached me from behind and asked. "Ready to go?"

"Yeah," I answered before I placed some flowers on each of the graves, then I got back to my feet, and walked away with Liam, a pleased smile on my face.

The ghosts of my past haunted me for so long. I was always looking back. Feeling as if I were trapped inside a cage of my own creation, yet I didn't have the key out.

But now, I was finally enjoying the simple pleasures of existence. I could finally wake up and actually be excited about what the day had to offer.

I was finally looking forward to the future. And I could not be happier to experience all of that with Liam because he was the one who made me want to look for the key and break free.

And now I could finally say that I had set myself free.

9 781944 253530